Soul of Flame

Wiccan Haus Book 15

By
Merryn Dexter

Copyright © 2016 by Merryn Dexter
ISBN: 978-1-68361-060-1
Cover art by Mina Carter

Published by
Decadent Publishing Company, LLC

Look for us online at:
www.decadentpublishing.com

Welcome to the Wiccan Haus

Something wiccan this way comes to a mystical mysterious island where authors get to play and bring their love stories to life. At the Wiccan Haus you will meet Rekkus, Cyrus, Sage, Sarka, Cemil and Myron, all of whom return in most if not all the stories. Yes each one will eventually get their HEA as well.

We hope you enjoy the stories from all the authors and return time and again to keep up with the staff and meet new characters along the way. But fear not if this is your first or twenty-first story each book stands on its own..

~A Note from the Author~

Welcome back to Wiccan Haus. I am delighted to share the story of Ceara and Shim with you. From the moment Dominique Eastwick invited me through the portal, I knew this magical island off the coast of Maine would be home to my imagination. It is an honor and a privilege to play in this fabulous world with so many authors who I admire and respect.

I am so pleased to work with the amazing Decadent Publishing team – dreams really do come true! My imagination is fired up so I hope to be able to bring you many more stories in partnership with them.

I would be thrilled to hear from you about this book, Wiccan Haus, the Black Hills Wolves, soup recipes, holidays, or anything else that crosses your mind. I'm a military spouse currently resident in Belgium and working from home so always happy for a distraction!

You can email me at merryn.dexter@yahoo.com or find me on Facebook or Twitter @MerrynDexter . I also have a website www.merryndexter.com and a blog www.merryndexter.blogspot.be

Best Wishes,
Merryn x

Dedication

For M. Who brings a little bit of magic into my life every day

When sundered soul is frozen and the black beast tamed to her hand
So will hearts unite and destiny be fulfilled.
All hail Queen of Clan, Mistress of All, Ruler of the Emerald Lands!

Prophecy of Aislinn the Touched—later called Aislinn the Mute—Lady of the Emerald Court.

Prologue

Ceara Smith adjusted the headset her point man Kellan hooked over her ears. Strapping herself into her allocated seat on the chopper, she tried to contain her building excitement. It had been too long since she'd walked in her element. While the rest of the crew piled in around her, she did a quick mic test and got the thumbs-up from Matthews, their team leader. Unlike the rest of them, who'd dressed in thick protective gear, Ceara wore a cotton top and pants and simple slip-on shoes.

Derren Williams, the last member to board, took the abusive banter from the rest with a customary one-fingered salute and winked at Ceara. She blew him a kiss in return which he snatched from the air and tucked into the front pocket of his Kevlar vest. Whistles and jeers echoed through her earphones, and she laughed.

"Wheels up," Matthews shouted.

The noise died down, and an air of quiet anticipation settled over the group. The chopper rose into the air, the sharp angle feeding the butterflies in Ceara's stomach. Static buzzed in her ears, and she looked toward Matthews. Their leader commanded the small space, his air of authority combat earned and hardened over years of experience. The grizzled man hooked his hands through a couple of support straps, bracing his booted feet wide apart. He cut an imposing figure, the edges of his close-cropped hair peppered with silver.

"Okay, here's what we know so far. Our target is a residential school on the outskirts of D.C. There's no indication yet on the source of the fire, but it's spreading fast. I've got reports of multiple groups of children trapped." He glanced around the group. "I know this is an unusual assignment, but it's an elite prep school. We're talking children of politicians, diplomats, senior officers. When the big dogs bark, we wag our tails and say 'Yes, sir!'"

Williams howled, a couple of the others barked and yipped. Matthews shook his head and retook his seat, but he didn't stop them from messing around.

Ceara smiled but didn't join in. *Soon, soon.* Knowing she would soon be inside the fire filled her with guilty pleasure. She hated and loved her job in equal measures. Their elite rescue squad only got summoned to life-threatening situations, but it meant she would be in her element.

Matthews held up his hand to signal five minutes from touchdown. The team fell silent, and Ceara closed her eyes, trying to relax. She hated the chopper, hated to be enclosed in so much metal, but she'd grown accustomed to it over the past century— the human world expanding its technology, and iron and steel springing up everywhere. She could withstand more than the average fae, her tolerance levels much higher. Being banished from her clan left little choice other than to adapt.

Her initial attempts to seek refuge in a number of other fae clans when she and her twin sister, Isolde, had first been banished, were all rebuffed. None accepted her, wary of attracting the legendary wrath of her clan queen. Having little in common with her twin, either in nature or in power, Ceara tried her best to blend into the mundane world of the humans. After many years, she'd found some semblance of peace and satisfaction in her life.

The whine of the rotors changed pitch, and she responded to the tap on her shoulder from Kellan beside her. She leaned across his lap to look out of the window, and her pulse raced at her first glimpse of the inferno below. A quick flick released her restraints the moment the chopper touched down, and she flowed from the machine like water, the lure of the flames crying out to her soul.

Matthews peeled away, heading for the temporary command post. Ceara held her position in the center of the formation, keeping easy pace with the group in spite of her height and weight difference to the huge men who encircled her. A black cap sat snug over her head, concealing her bright-red hair, which would draw curious eyes. Matthews signaled for the others to approach the central block of the school. The four-story U-shaped monstrosity loomed before them, complete with Doric columns and a sweeping driveway.

Heat enveloped her like a lover's caress, teasing the perpetual cold from her skin. The men paused to lower their face shields. Impatience raked through her, and she bounced on her toes at the delay. *They're only human.* Moving as one, they crossed the gravel driveway, fanning out to form an inverted V with Ceara taking point. Kellan stood behind her, taking the discarded items when she tugged off her hat and kicked free of her thin shoes.

Flames roared from the doorway, a siren's call. Running barefoot up the stairs, she dove into the fire. The thin clothing she wore burned away in moments, leaving her naked. She threw her arms open, welcoming the flickering heat dancing over her skin. Energy flooded into her body, chasing off any lingering weakness from her exposure to the alien technologies of the human world. The flames leaped forward to greet her, licking at her skin like eager puppies. She wanted to play, wanted to dance and twirl through the fire, but lives were at stake. She snapped her fingers, and the flames fell back.

The blaze in the main foyer died down, and the team would pound through the open doorway any moment. Professional as they were, her naked body would be an unnecessary distraction to them. Stroking her hands over her head, she summoned the fire, turning her hair from red into living flame. Repeating the gesture at her breasts and hips, she coated her flesh in bands of blazing orange and red.

Kellan pounded up the stairs, the rest hard on his heels. The huge man bent forward. "Boss says the dorms in the west wing have all been evacuated," he said in her ear. "Top floor of the east still has some kids trapped. They're not sure on numbers yet, still struggling for a head count, but that's where he wants us to focus."

With a quick nod, she climbed the stairs, pushing back the flames to clear a safe path. The heat from the fire poured into her, and she welcomed it.

They headed straight to the top floor and commenced a methodical sweep of the rooms. Standing in the center of each room, she called the heat and flames to her, feeding her soul as the others fanned out to check closets and underneath beds. They came up empty again and again, and she frowned at Kellan who shrugged, lifting the mic attached to his protective headgear.

"Boss double-checking the info on east." He paused to listen. "They've got kids from this area unaccounted for, Ceara. We keep searching." The uneasy look on his face echoed her own doubts, but second-guessing orders got people killed. She respected Matthews, trusted him. He'd proved time and time again the welfare of his crew was his utmost priority.

They pressed on down the length of the corridor, checking every room but finding nothing. They used the stairwell at the far corner to enter the third floor, and Ceara held up a hand to keep the men back. She slipped through the door. Flames surged, hungry to feed on the fresh oxygen. Striding down the corridor, she clenched her fists, drawing down the fire. Pleasure shuddered through her, the intense heat engulfing her senses. *Talk to me. Show me where the source is.* Thick smoked billowed out into the stairwell behind her.

Opening herself wider to the flames, she pulled them into her, sucking the heat into the core of her being. The fire pulled back for the first time, as if drawn to a magnet of stronger polarity. She held her ground. There was no fire in the human realm capable of resisting her for long. Absorbing the heat and flames, she consumed the blaze until the smoke lessened and she could see the team framed in the opening.

At her nod, they entered the corridor, repeating the sweep from downstairs until they came to one room they couldn't open. She signaled them to hold again. Her nose wrinkled; a faint smell of sulfur lingered beneath the scents of smoke and ash. The door had been sealed with more than just a key. Focusing on the lock, she sent out a tiny thread of flame, using it to unknot the spell holding it secure.

When it at last fell loose, she eased the door open. A group of a dozen or so children stared back at her, and she breathed a sigh of relief. Turning aside, she let the team enter, and they escorted the children out, following the cleared path she held in the fire and down the stairwell. Kellen stood in front of her, shielding her from the children's curious gazes.

"Hey, Blaze. There's something seriously weird about this room."

Ceara smiled at the nickname and peered around Kellen's broad shoulder to get a better view. She frowned. The room lay untouched by fire, not even a smudge of soot on the walls. Heart in her mouth, she stepped inside.

She studied the walls in growing horror. Garlands of sweet, sunny, bright-yellow flowers, knotted together, hung from the walls. She cried out, falling to her knees. A blast of flame flew from her fingers, igniting a pile of books, and the fire spread, eager to consume this new source of fuel.

"Blaze, honey, what's wrong?" Kellen crouched next to her.

She screamed, scrambling backward. "Get out, Kell! Get out, for the love of the Lord and Lady, you must run! Faebane!"

Ceara shuddered, her control slipping, the floor around her starting to burn. Kellen recoiled from the curtain of heat encircling her. The well of flames inside her twisted, blistering through her veins. She screamed in agony.

"Run, Kell! Run, please!" Sobbing, she fought to hold in the flames.

Boots pounded on the tiled floor, and Ceara counted at a measured pace, battling against the power of the trap. The fire swelled, creating a pressure unlike anything she'd ever experienced.

"Lord and Lady, save them," she whispered over and over, trying in vain to contain the heat.

Tension eased in Matthews's gut as his guys

appeared, escorting a small group of children. The local police rushed forward and wrapped the kids in foil blankets, herding them behind the safe cordon. His men didn't hesitate, plunging back inside the burning building. "What's the head count now?" he snapped at the coordinator, snarling in disgust when the fool hesitated. *Fucking amateurs.* Two more minutes and he would call them back, regardless.

A roar from the east wing drowned out the noise of the crying children. Horror clenched his guts, turning them to water. The fire at the windows sucked inward, the sudden darkness blinding him for a second. The world paused for a single heartbeat before a huge explosion ripped through the wing, blowing the roof off and sending glass and debris flying. A concussive shockwave knocked him on his ass, leaving him gasping for breath.

He struggled to his feet, ears ringing, throat parched and aching. A few ruined timbers stuck up from the pile of debris, the twisted limbs all that remained of the building. A few wisps of smoke twisted into the air, but the flames were gone. Matthews dropped to his knees, tears pouring down his cheeks. *My team!*

Chapter One

Ceara huddled in the corner of the ferry, tugging her thick jacket closer around herself. Her teeth chattered from the relentless cold. She hadn't been able to get warm since waking the previous week in the private hospital ward. The nurses' whispers about a miraculous recovery made her want to laugh in their faces. Her corporeal form may have survived, but that was all. The fire had vanished, leaving her soul empty, void.

Matthews had paid her a visit and confirmed what she already knew. The entire team had died, killed by her inability to control the fire. He'd asked her what went wrong, but she'd refused to answer. The boss knew more than he should already about the existence of the fae, and she wouldn't do anything else to put him in danger.

She had lain in the sterile, white room for days without speaking, and Matthews had returned that morning with a ticket and a bagful of clothes and essentials. He'd threatened to dress her himself if she didn't cooperate. Bundling her into his car, he drove for a couple of hours, heading toward the coast. Ignoring her protests, he shoved her onto the small ferry without explanation.

Ceara had a feeling she knew her destination, although she could not understand how she'd been gifted with a ticket. Wiccan Haus was renowned throughout the para realms. The ferry she rode carried human guests—all paras arrived and departed the island via one of the portals. She looked around at the other passengers who hung from the rail, straining for a glimpse of the island. Chatter about the resort milled through the group. They discussed the classes each wanted to take, but she refused all attempts to be drawn into conversation. Tugging her jacket hood up, she shoved her gloved hands deep into her pockets.

Conversation faded, quieting beneath the blanket of fog enveloping the small vessel. The sun disappeared, the temperature plummeting, and she shivered in earnest. Pain racked her body, and she bent double, squeezing her eyes shut. The cold struck deep, and concerned murmurs about the sudden fog bank rose around her.

The sounds of distress faded once the ferry broke through the wet, dank curtain and the sun blazed again. The cabin emptied, the other guests hurrying to lean over the side rails, gasping and exclaiming at their first sight of the island.

White cliffs rose high, trees dotted the landscape, and the very tips of the Haus could be seen peeking through the woods. A natural harbor carved deep into the cliff held a loading dock, and a few small boats bobbed in the gentle ripples made by the ferry as it edged closer to dry land.

The ferry bumped against the dock. She barely registered the movement as she shuddered in the corner, until a soft touch on her shoulder stilled the pain in her body. Blinking back tears, she stared into a pair of bright-blue eyes. A tall man with flowing blond hair leaned over her, and she recognized him as one of the Rowan siblings, the owners of Wiccan Haus and the island upon which it sat.

"Be well, Ceara. I am Cemil Rowan and you are welcome at Wiccan Haus." The man wrapped a heated blanket around her shivering form, coaxing her from the cabin to the gangplank leading from the ferry to the pier. She clutched the cozy material close, shuffling along the strip of wood. Cemil followed her, his heavy tread making the plank bounce beneath her feet.

The Haus rose ahead of her, its wooden chalet-style architecture both quirky and welcoming. She followed Cemil on the short walk to reception, keeping her eyes on the path beneath her feet. Although the day was pleasant, Ceara gained no comfort from the sun. She didn't think she would ever be warm again. The blanket eased the worst of her shivers, but could do nothing to fill the aching cold in her soul.

Cemil paused at the entrance to the Haus, a kind smile on his face. "We will find a way to heal you, Ceara. Have a little faith in us."

With no time for platitudes, she brushed past him into the foyer. "The Lord and Lady are silent to me, Cemil. My powers are spent, and I am naught but a husk, doomed to eternity with no purpose, no calling. I have heard many stories of the Rowans and your abilities, but some things are beyond your ken."

She waited at the reception desk, studying the young woman seated behind it who shuffled a pack of cards, her entire focus on them as she dealt four face up before her. *This child may be human but not mundane.* The young woman lifted her head and smiled. Her nametag said "Cyrus" which Ceara found confusing to say the least. The woman brushed her turquoise bangs from her forehead and tilted her head to one side, studying her.

"Well, you are a conundrum, aren't you? A para without power. Every time I ask the cards for your room number it comes up with something different. I'm not sure what to do with you. My instincts say second floor, but it doesn't sit well to place you amongst the other paras when you are defenseless. A room number for the third floor comes up two out of three times, but what risk to the human residents should you regain your power and become unstable?" The small woman frowned past Ceara's shoulder.

"What's the problem, Myron?" Cemil's easygoing tone and relentless good nature irritated Ceara.

The small woman opened her mouth to explain, but a deep, growling voice cut across her.

"The problem, Cemil, is you permitted a para to approach the island via the ferry, and you didn't bother to clue me in." A huge man, well over six feet tall, folded his arms across his broad chest and glared at Ceara as though all of this was her fault. His deep voice held a lyrical quality, and she surmised he'd once called one of the Celtic lands home. "I'm head of security in case you'd bloody forgotten. How the hell can I be expected to protect the family and residents of the island if you don't keep me informed?" His voice deepened further, the contained power and grace of his posture screaming shifter.

"She needed our help, Rekkus. Without her powers, she is no threat to the humans. Sage and I discussed it and agreed her need for healing outweighed your rules. Expecting her to travel unprotected through the para realms is unreasonable." Cemil paused and studied Ceara with a shrewd look. "Her obligation to a human friend is the only reason she came to us. I doubt she would be here without his perseverance."

Ceara ducked her head, refusing to acknowledge the truth in the Wiccan's observant words. Another dark-haired man joined the group, and she sighed at the growing audience. She didn't even want to be here in the first place, never mind be the source of so much unwanted attention. The newcomer resembled Cemil, although everything about him was dark—his hair, his clothing, even the leather gloves he wore.

She moved away from the desk area, giving the staff space to have a heated discussion about security and accommodation. Turning in a slow circle, she examined the rafters of the airy space. Wood surrounded her, the sort of environment that would sing to her powers, rich with sources of fuel, but her soul lay dead inside her. A small blonde woman hurried through the front door, her long skirt billowing. She adjusted a large cloth bag over her shoulder. Smiling sweetly, as though they were old friends, she held out her hands in greeting.

"Ceara, it's good to have you with us. I've just finished preparing your cottage, and I'm sure you will enjoy the location. It's not far from the meadow, which will be one of the spaces we use for your healing." Sage—who else could it be, with blonde hair and sparkling blue eyes so like Cemil's—waved toward the group at the desk as she hurried to the elevators. "Can one of you get Ceara settled in the stone cottage? I must check the humans are all resting before the portal opens." With a smile and a waft of lavender and thyme, the beautiful young woman disappeared into the far right elevator.

Cemil grinned and shrugged at the frowning security officer and the silent, black-clad man beside him. "It seems Sage has it all in hand. I'll take our guest to the cottage. I'm sure you will want to monitor the rest of the para arrivals."

The big man growled viciously, snatching his clipboard from the reception desk. "I can't bloody wait to see what surprises come through that damn portal."

The picturesque path led from the Haus to the meadow, and Cemil, a conscientious guide, pointed out various routes leading from the main pathway—to the south, a wooded area surrounded a lake. To the north lay an orchard, the faint scent of apple blossom traveling on the air. She listened to the information and instructions he gave. They passed a set of gates, which he indicated was the entrance to the meadow, and the path continued up to the northwest, growing steeper. A narrow trail appeared to the left, winding through the trees, and he guided her along it. Just a few paces in, the trees opened onto a delightful bower with a grassed area and a single-story stone cottage on one side, pale gray with a darker slate roof. The door stood ajar.

Cemil pushed open the door. Ducking his head beneath the frame, he entered the living space. The open-plan area featured a large plush couch before a huge brick fireplace which blazed away in spite of the warmth of the day. At the back of the room stood an enormous bed, dressed in crisp, cream cotton sheets with a thick dark-green blanket rolled back at the foot. A set of gauzy curtains were hooked back and would provide a semblance of privacy for the bed area when released from their position. A stone archway to the right led to a bathroom with a luxury shower stall and a huge sunken bath, carved from the same stone as the cottage itself. Candles ringed the edge of the tub, and a large basket on the counter held a selection of soaps and shampoos.

"Sage makes those specifically for each guest." Cemil lifted one of the bars to his nose and inhaled. "Ginger and pink peppercorns, a perfect combination for a salamander."

"Do not call me that," she snapped. Snatching her bag away from his grasp, she headed over to the large bed.

"My apologies, Ceara, but your current difficulties do not mean you should deny your very self." He approached the door, pausing in the entranceway to regard her. "The portal will open soon. You will hear it and no doubt feel the vibrations. Rest and get settled in, but don't forget you must return to the Haus for dinner. All our guests dine together, without exception." With that final instruction, he departed, the cottage seeming empty without his presence.

The crackling of the logs in the fireplace drew and repelled her in equal measures. She edged closer to the warmth of the fire to examine the sideboard holding an electric kettle, a mug tree, and a small wooden box. Prying open the lid, she bent her head to draw in the delicious scents of the homemade infusions encased in small muslin bags.

She brewed a cup of tea and perched cross-legged on the dark-green velvet couch, her gaze resting time and again on the flickering flames. Her cheeks flushed, the warmth from the fire heating up the room. The smoky lapsang souchong and orange tea spread an echoing warmth in her belly, and she uncurled her limbs as the bone-deep chill loosened.

Ceara unzipped her jacket and pulled the hood back. Her once-vibrant red hair fell in a limp brown mass around her shoulders, and she leaned back deeper into the plump cushions.

The muted tones of the cottage provided a pleasant contrast to the harsh brightness of the clinic room she'd occupied for the previous few weeks, which seemed half a world away already. How had Matthews been able to arrange for her passage to the island?

Thoughts of their stoic leader led to memories of the rest of her team, and fat tears rolled down her cheeks. Staring into the dancing flames, she pictured Kellan, Derren, and the others writhing in agony as her failed control incinerated them to ash and bone.

Chapter Two

Shimeer Neguar waited at the instructed entry point, flipping the small, bright-red lizard-shaped charm in his hand. The shape of the charm meant nothing to him, black jaguars having little in common with lizards too small to even be considered snack worthy. The ground beneath his feet shuddered, but Shim held steady, unlike some of the others who queued beside him. Living at the foot of a volcano deep in the Ecuadorian rainforest, he'd gotten used to Mother Earth shrugging her shoulders.

A low rumble built until a loud boom rolled around the platform, and the portal appeared before him. Shim slung his duffel bag over his shoulder and stepped through, his alpha nature making it impossible for him to cede to any of his traveling companions. He entered a plain stone room, nodding in respect at the huge were-tiger who stood in front of him. Rekkus Duteigr, a legend among the big cat shifters. His reputation had spread even to the remote forest areas where Shim and his kind preferred to dwell. Rekkus was the last of his kind, the sole living black tiger—although rumors circulated of a recent mating.

Shim knew what it meant to be alone, the last

survivor of his clan. Other jaguar clans still existed in the depths of the rainforest, but none were related to him. Overtures had been made by a few who wanted him to join their prowl and refresh their bloodlines, but he had little interest in mating. Especially while he remained cursed. He loosed a coughing growl at the thought of his curse and the evil fae bitch who'd ruined his life. If he ever got his hands on her again....

A rumble from Rekkus brought him back to full awareness, and he ceased his own growling, raising a hand in apology. The head of security for the island squinted before gesturing another guard forward who escorted him to reception for his room allocation.

The pretty human female behind the desk gave him an appraising look, and he flashed her a quick smile. A tasty little morsel like her might be just what he needed to take his mind off the shit-fest he called life. He thought about the last female to catch his eye, shuddering at the echo of sharp, cold pain blasting through his shoulder. He rubbed the joint, a reflex action to soothe a wound long healed.

Claiming the key to his room, he listened to the strict instruction to use only the middle elevator which would take him to the second floor, reserved for the use of para species. With a quick nod, he strode across the lobby. The rest of the para guests gathered at the desk, and he was in no mood to be in a confined space with any of them.

A snake shifter hissed as he passed. He paused long enough to bare his teeth at the impudent fool before hitting the elevator and escaping the busy lobby for the peace and quiet of his room. Jaguars preferred to remain solitary. Being around crowds—particularly in unfamiliar territory—raised his hackles. The trip through the capital city to the portal had driven him near crazy with all the noises and smells.

The key to Room 2 slipped into the well-oiled lock, and he stepped inside the airy space. The furnishings were plain, sparse even, but perfect for his needs. A large bed dominated the area, and he dropped his duffel on the caramel-colored cover before stepping into the bathroom. The huge tub and multi-jet shower were a welcome sight, and he stripped his clothes before stepping into the glass stall, turning the jets on full blast. The hot water pounded his tense muscles, washing away the stink of the city. He grabbed a bar of dark-green soap from the rack. Eucalyptus and cloves filled the room, the steam absorbing and magnifying the scent. He drew in a huge lungful of hot air while scrubbing at his short black hair. The black-on-black rosettes decorating his fur in animal form were echoed in his human form, and, unlike some other shifters, his eyes stayed the same jade-green whether man or beast.

He dried off and regarded the bed, fighting the urge to take a nap and unwind from the stresses of the day. The instruction to attend dinner had been explicit, so he pulled his clothes out of the duffel and shoved them into the chest of drawers, keeping out a fresh shirt and jeans. Kicking his hated shoes under the bed, he strode barefoot from the room. With a few minutes before dinner started, he decided to explore the Haus and get his bearings. He palmed the small folding map he'd been issued with his room key and headed for the elevator.

Having spent longer than he intended poking his head into various treatment rooms, closets, and offices, Shim hurried into the dining room. He headed to the side painted dark-green, which his guide told him had been reserved for the para guests. Small tables and chairs scattered about the space, and he chose one by the window so he could keep the rest of the room in sight. He perused the menu and gave his order to the wait staff, accepting a jug of water with a nod. Alcohol was not available to guests, but he wasn't bothered. He wanted to keep his wits sharp until he could assess the other residents. He'd met the paranormal faction waiting for the portal to open, and, like him, none of them seemed inclined toward company. They ranged through the para-allocated section of the room, each at lone tables.

He turned his attention to the opposite side of the room, painted lighter-green and reserved for the human guests. They were a little more sociable, it seemed, a couple of larger tables occupied by small groups. A person sat alone, a small figure bundled in an oversized hooded sweatshirt, female by her stature.

As though feeling his eyes upon her, the woman raised her head, and he recoiled in horror. The face of his nightmares stared back at him, framed by the hood of the sweatshirt. Hatred boiling in his veins, he studied her high cheekbones, the same stubborn jawline he saw every night in his dreams. His chair flew in one direction, the table another. He yanked his shirt over his head then shed his jeans. Ignoring the gasps and wide-eyed stares from the humans, he focused on the bitch across the room. Crouching low, he let the shift come. Bones snapping and twisting, his jaguar forced his way to the fore in a shimmer of light. Huge leg muscles propelled him across the room in a matter of moments.

The woman stumbled from her seat, but he cut off her escape route. He paced closer, tail flicking, eyes locked on his prey. The woman tripped over the edge of one of the tables, falling backwards. Her hood slipped down, revealing dull-brown hair instead of the white-blonde he'd expected to see, but he didn't hesitate. Claws pricking deep, he pinned her limbs to the floor before she could summon her power. His fur started to itch and burn. He growled in frustration at the first signs of his curse taking effect. Adrenaline and fury had carried him through the change but, now, a thousand fire ants crawled beneath his skin.

Shaking his head to try and clear the tears in his eyes, he pressed his face close to the fae bitch. Saliva dripped from his open jaws to trickle down her neck. He snarled into her terrified face. The chocolate hue to her iris surprised him. It was not the cold blue he expected to see, but the fae were renowned for their trickery and glamor. Terror in those deep-brown depths melted first into resignation and then peace.

The screams and shouts behind him muted, a distant nuisance to be ignored. Though he longed to savor the moment of his revenge, a security team would arrive any moment and spoil his fun. He'd spent too many days plotting what he would do if he ever got his claws into her again. He would not be thwarted.

The slender fae turned her head, exposing her long pale neck, and he pressed close, expecting the bitter icy scent he despised. The lungful of warm smoke and spice he inhaled made him lightheaded. Soft, creamy skin exposed when she turned her head begged for his bite. He spread his jaws wide, preparing to sink his teeth deep to rend her flesh, but the urge to lick her overwhelmed him.

Shim pulled back, staring at her, wary as the woman turned her head to regard him. She looked so familiar, and yet not.

The pain beneath his skin itched beyond his ability to bear, and tears poured from his eyes. A tickling sensation built in his throat and nose until he couldn't hold it in. A sharp pain in his side distracted a moment before he let loose an almighty sneeze straight into her face. Huge hands grappled around his throat and rolled him off his prey.

He couldn't struggle against the hands gripping him, his muscles like water. Rekkus' face loomed close, twisted into a harsh snarl. He pulled back a meaty fist and punched Shim in the jaw. The blow combined with the sedative pumping through his veins from the dart gun, and he slumped to the floor.

His eyes flickered closed, and he battled to open them, his vision blurred by a combination of the drugs and his tears. The fae sat up, her face twisted in utter disgust. Lifting her hand, she tried to remove a huge lump of snot from her hair. Her face dripped with it, and he curled his lip in a smile.

That'll teach the bitch to curse me into being allergic to my animal form.

Blackness swallowed him.

Chapter Three

Ceara wiped her face with the thick, white towel Cyrus handed to her. He crouched close, shielding her from view. The Light Ones moved around the room, settling the other guests, their calm, sweet natures being more suitable to the task. Sage whipped up a batch of shakes as Cemil wove a tale about an accidental escape from the preserve, the island's own animal sanctuary.

Desperate for a shower, she struggled to her feet. The mucus in her hair set like glue, and a cold trail ran down her neck into her bra. Trying not to retch at the unpleasant sensation, she followed the Dark Ones, as Cyrus and his sister Sarka were known, from the room. Shock turned to irritation when they led her to an office behind the reception desk. She wanted nothing more than to seek the sanctuary of her cottage. The pair studied her from the other side of the desk, their icy-blue eyes an unwelcome reminder of her twin, although the emotion reflected by the Rowans appeared sympathetic—something she'd never seen in her sister's gaze.

"Do you require medical assistance?" Sarka asked, and Ceara shook her head. Her arms stung a little from scratches left by the jaguar's claws, but if she never saw a medic again it would be too soon.

She'd experienced a moment of utter peace pinned beneath the big cat. Waiting for those sharp fangs to sink deep into her throat, she'd blessed the Fates for providing a release. She longed for nothing more than to escape the prison her life had become since the fire went silent. Hot fury surged in her veins at the Wiccans and their staff for interfering, although she fought hard not to show it.

"And you're sure you've never met Shimeer Neguar before?" Cyrus sounded somewhat skeptical. *Who is this impudent pup to question my honesty?* The fae were skilled at manipulating the truth, but she'd grown out of the habit after spending so long away from court.

"I have never seen him until a few moments ago. The majority of the past century, I have dwelled in the mundane world. I assume you are aware of my banishment?" She raised one eyebrow at Cyrus, and he nodded.

"We ran a check on you with the Syndicate prior to your arrival." He pinched the bridge of his nose with one gloved hand, frowning. *I'm not going to like this.*

"Unbeknownst to us, your clan queen left a standing instruction with them. Any inquiries regarding you or your sister are to be reported to her. I've pulled some strings, and they've agreed to keep it quiet until the end of the week. Given the little I know of fae politics, you must have done something special to get banished?"

Her stomach roiled at the unwelcome news. Taking a deep breath, she held it for a moment. Regardless of her current lack of power, she was still one of the Shining Ones and not the weak human she'd pretended to be. Forcing her shoulders back, posture ramrod straight, she regarded the siblings.

"The queen believes my twin, Isolde, and I are

the subjects of prophecy. It predicts she will be overthrown by whichever of us fulfills the terms." She snorted softly before continuing. "Unlike my sister, I have zero interest in taking over one of the fae clans. I cannot imagine anything worse than trying to rule such a duplicitous group as my extended family."

A gleam of interest sparked in Sarka's eyes.

Ceara shook her head. "I will not discuss this further with you. I am not the one referred to in the prophecy. And I have no more to say on the matter."

The siblings exchanged a long look. *Do they share some kind of telepathic link?*

A sharp rap at the door announced the arrival of Rekkus. The big man looked furious as he shot Ceara an apologetic glance.

"Ms. Smith, I'm sorry about what happened. The minute the portal opens at sunup, your assailant will be removed from the island. He's under guard now and will remain so until his departure."

The were-tiger took up more than his fair share of space. She slid from her chair to ensure a clear access route to the open door. His golden eyes tracked her every move, but she shrugged off the sensation of being hunted. She was not prey to be watched. Lifting her chin, she straightened, wishing she wore something other than jeans and layers of shirts.

"Did the jaguar tell you why he attacked me?" Steel laced her voice, and Rekkus squared his shoulders. *That's right. I am not some plaything awaiting your tender mercies, shifter.*

"He's confused and in a lot of pain. Claims you cursed him after he escaped from you. He kept calling you the Ice Bitch, which doesn't make much sense to me. Cemil told me your affinity is to fire." Rekkus scowled then shrugged. "Whatever, he attacked you and we don't stand for that here. I'm kicking his arse straight back through the portal and that's all there is to it."

Ice Bitch struck such a cord, and she struggled to keep her face neutral. The red-rimmed jade eyes of the huge black jaguar loomed large in her mind. The words of the prophecy rose unbidden, *and the black beast tamed to her hand....*

Is it possible Isolde captured Shimeer, believing him to be the black beast? Her twin had never lacked ambition. She acted without conscience when it came to any being she deemed less than her, which covered pretty much every living soul, para and human.

If there was one thing Isolde wasn't short on, it was ego.

"I think the jaguar made an honest mistake. He could have killed me before you managed to subdue him, but he did not. If he is suffering under a curse, then he should be offered the chance of healing. Provided he stays away from me, I have no problem with him remaining on the island."

Sarka twisted her hair into a knot behind her head before sighing and shaking it down to flow freely again. She turned her frowning gaze from Ceara to Cyrus. "If the jaguar is cursed, then we'll need to consult Janessa. You need to question him, Cy. Find out everything he knows about what happened to him." She made notes, and her brother peered over her shoulder, adding a comment here and there.

A loud rumble filled the room, drawing everyone's attention to Rekkus. His golden eyes glowing hot and furious, he spoke in a low growl. "In case you've all forgotten, I'm the head of bloody security, and it's up to me who stays on the island. I can't have guests attacking each other. If we make an exception for the jaguar, it'll be a damned bloodbath."

Cyrus grinned at Rekkus, ripped the list of scribbled questions from his sister's notepad, and crossed the room. He clapped his best friend on the shoulder and steered him toward the door. "I'm sure you can find a suitable punishment. Aren't you the least bit curious, old friend? We haven't had a decent curse to deal with in ages. I'm dying to get to the bottom of it. What do you say?"

Rekkus growled but allowed himself to be led from the room. "I say curiosity killed the frigging cat, which is all right for you but a gigantic pain in the arse for me!"

Ceara lay submerged in the huge bathtub, the scalding water up to her nose. She'd taken a shower to wash off the unmentionable crap the jaguar sneezed into her face and hair and now relaxed in the herb-filled water. Sarka had given her a potion, promising it would help her to sleep. She'd included some warming properties when she noticed her constant shivering. The hot bath chased off the worst of the cold, but it couldn't touch the frozen void in her chest since the fire abandoned her. Sighing, she ducked her head under the water, bored with the endless pity party of her thoughts.

She couldn't leave the island until the end of the week. The ferry wouldn't return before then, and she did not relish the thought of using the portal and ending up helpless in the para realm. Two options remained—sit around and sulk for the rest of the week, or make the most of the island's facilities. Thinking about the island reminded her why she was there. She owed it to Matthews to try. He should have left her to rot after her actions caused the deaths of the rest of their close-knit team. Pushing his grief aside, he'd done everything possible to ensure her survival. *You're the only family left to me, girl.*

She held little hope the Rowans could reignite her power, but a few relaxation classes might help to regain some balance. The peace and quiet would also give her time to decide what to do next. Massaging shampoo into her scalp, she recalled the sensation of the jaguar's breath on her throat. So close to oblivion and escape from her pain, but if the Lord and Lady had deemed her worthy of release, she would not have survived the detonation of her powers in the first place.

It was also the coward's way out, something she'd never been. She hadn't learned to survive in a clan of the Unseelie Court by being weak or hiding from the truth about herself. Ambivalence was the most charitable emotion when it came to her family. She had no desire to return to the endless political machinations of court, but she would not deny her heritage. Isolde embodied the darker side of their upbringing, developing both a ruthless ambition and a taste for pain. Ceara did what she needed to get by and avoid being a victim, but the power games bored her, and she'd been happy to keep a low profile.

The Unseelie Court was divided into many different clans, formed from familial and political connections. Each clan adopted a jewel name, the Diamond Clan being the uppermost and seat of the high queen. Ceara and her sister had been born into the Emerald Clan.

The words of the prophecy played through her mind. *When sundered soul is frozen and the black beast tamed to her hand, so will hearts unite and destiny be fulfilled. All hail Queen of Clan, Mistress of All, Ruler of the Emerald Lands!*

Growing up as a twin, Isolde had fixated on the sundered-soul reference, her power designation ice to Ceara's fire. It appeared her sister had spent her time in banishment hunting down a para who would meet the black beast criteria, and Shimeer was the unlucky recipient of her attentions. Given the jaguar's reaction, Isolde hadn't been too successful in uniting their hearts.

Wrapping her hair in a thick towel, Ceara bundled herself into a pair of thick flannel pajamas. She loaded more wood onto the fire blazing in the hearth then drank the potion from Sarka. Relishing the heat spreading in her belly, she climbed into the large bed. The wooden frame, like almost everything in the cottage, was made of natural materials. Whoever prepared the cottage for her arrival had made sure to avoid iron and steel items, whenever possible. A simple thing, perhaps, but it showed the effort the Rowans put into tailoring each guest's environment to their specific needs.

Her lids flickered closed, and a pair of jade-green eyes burned in her mind's eye. Drifting away, a thought teased her mind. For those few moments the jaguar pinned her to the ground, she hadn't been the least bit cold.

Chapter Four

S him stared in disquiet at the Spartan room the security guards dragged him into. The effects of the tranquilizer still messed with his system, leaving him no choice but to sit on the edge of the plain hard bed, one of the few features in the unadorned room.

The door slammed behind him, and a thick bar slid into place, sealing Shim into the small room. His nose twitched in disgust. The place smelled like wet dog and hormones. It would be full moon in two days and the barracks were occupied. Crossing the room on unsteady feet, he put his face against the doorframe and drew in a deep breath. Tasting the musky scents, he identified wolves and a bear...no cats, though, other than a faint trace of Rekkus lingering in the air.

Staggering to the bed, he lay on his back, hands pillowed beneath his head. He stared at the whitewashed ceiling. The other occupants were of no concern to him, a bunch of hormonal teens struggling to come to terms with the pull of the moon. The island provided a safe refuge and training facility for young weres who couldn't control themselves. They rotated through every month around the full moon until they grew mature enough to handle themselves in their animal forms, when the power of the goddess heated their blood.

The ebb and flow of the moon called to all her shifter children, but it had been many years since he'd been prone to the bouts of insane lust the scent of a female could provoke when the goddess rode high. A waft of smoke-and-spice tickled his memory. Shim growled, picturing a creamy swan neck lying bare before his jaws.

Some fae could cast a glamor to alter their features. He'd assumed that was the case when encountering his nemesis earlier. Very few possessed the strength to twist their own scent, though—maybe a handful across both courts. The bitch had never done it during his captivity, and she'd tried everything to possess him. He'd found her bitter scent so repugnant, her repeated attempts at seduction failed to raise an erection. He snarled at the thought of her cold little hands manipulating his flesh, the inevitable anger and punishment meted out when his body failed to respond.

A loud bang stirred him from his thoughts. The door flew open, and the glowering form of Rekkus filled the entire entrance. Forcing himself to stay in his relaxed position, he shackled his screaming cat. The human side of him knew they were still too weak from the tranquilizer. The odds of him beating Rekkus in a straight fight, even at full strength, were slim at best.

The tiger had a fearsome reputation. A highly skilled fighter, taller and heavier than Shim in both forms. The one advantage Shim had lay in the compression strength of his jaguar bite, but he couldn't see Rekkus letting him close enough to get a decent grip with his jaws. He also had nothing against the tiger, not even the tooth-rattling punch in the jaw. He'd been doing his job. Shim had violated the sanctity of Wiccan Haus through his violent actions.

"She all right?" He didn't know where the question came from. He didn't give a shit about the fae bitch, did he?

Rekkus raised one dark eyebrow, turning sideways to allow Cyrus to slip into the room. The dark man tapped his gloved finger against his lip, examining Shim like a bug under a microscope. Shim locked his spine tight, determined to maintain his relaxed facade.

"Ceara is as well as can be expected under the circumstances," Cyrus said in a soft voice. "But I'm not here to talk about her. I want to talk about your curse."

Shim snorted. "We can't exactly talk about my curse without talking about the bitch who placed it on me, can we?" Abandoning the pretense of calm, he rolled to his feet, pacing two strides back and forth beside the bed. His cat forced him into motion. The memories of those hellish six months, never far from the surface, bubbled up one after the other.

Phantom pain struck his shoulders and hips where spears of ice had pinned him to the floor of an isolated frozen cave. His back itched, not from the vestiges of the curse, but from remembered pain when he'd ripped his skin off, tearing free from the ice-covered floor.

A snarl built in the back of his throat. The jaguar pressed forward, wanting to shift so he could protect them both. He battled it down—there was no sanctuary or safety in his animal form anymore. He wanted to throw his head back and scream at the agony of such loss.

"She's not who you think she is, Shimeer." Cyrus' cool tone calmed him, even as the words increased his confusion. His head snapped up, his eyes locking with the Wiccan's.

"What do you know about it? What has she told you?" He couldn't keep the snarl from his voice. Stomach churning, he feared the worst. Feared his shame was no longer secret. Swallowing down the bile in the back of his throat, he waited for humiliation to strike.

"Ceara's affinity is to fire."

He laughed. There was nothing warm about the ice bitch; she was playing the Rowans for a fool.

"Her twin sister is another story. It would appear their powers are opposites—fire and ice," Rekkus interjected.

Shim opened his mouth, closed it as he tried to absorb the information then opened it again to argue. Cyrus held up one leather-gloved hand to forestall him. "I have spoken to a representative of the Syndicate, and they have verified this. You owe Ceara an apology, although you may have to put it in writing. She has requested we keep you away from her for the rest of the week. She is a guest here, too, and requires our aid."

Shim sank to the side of the bed, covering his face with his hands. *How is this possible? What kind of cruel trick do the Fates play on me now?*

He wanted nothing more than to roam his territory in freedom. He kept an eye on the local tribes, protected the land from too much incursion by the tourists visiting the Poás Volcano National Park. The tribes worshipped his clan as gods, but the Neguars had never exploited them. Family ties loosened over the years, driven by their solitary natures. Connections faded and their numbers shrank. His parents had been the last breeding pair of their clan.

He raised his eyes to the watchful pair. "What's wrong with her?"

Rekkus just folded his arms and gave him a look that clearly said *mind your own fucking business*.

He tried a different tack. "You are sure she's not here because of me?"

Cyrus looked thoughtful for a moment. "She's here because she was involved in an accident. We will be assisting with her recovery."

Which doesn't answer my question at all.

Scooting back on the bed, he crossed his legs in front of him. Time to forget about the little fae and focus on his own problems. "A fae captured me, held me against my will. She tortured me with ice because I wouldn't give her what she wanted. I waited for my opportunity, and, the instant she let her guard down, I attacked her. She bargained her life for my freedom." Drawing in a shuddering breath, he rolled his shoulders trying to relieve some of the tension racking his body.

"What did she want from you?" Rekkus murmured, a dangerous hint in his voice.

Shim didn't want to tell the tiger what he already suspected. He didn't want his suffering to stir up bad memories for Rekkus. The sad history of the last of the black tigers served as a warning to the other shifters. Rekkus' father had force-bonded his mother, leading to her madness and the destruction of the rest of the family at her hand.

Shim studied his own hands, balled in tight fists resting on top of his thighs. "She tried to force a mating," he whispered. The fury and despair in the snarl loosed from Rekkus, echoed his own.

"And the curse?" Cyrus prompted, turning the conversation back on track.

Shim nodded in gratitude and carried on talking. "I made her take me to the outskirts of the capital city. I knew I could get help there to find my way home. I didn't want her anywhere near my lands. She wore a necklace, a talisman of some type she used to teleport between locations. I don't know where she got it, but she would come and go, leaving me alone for days at a time."

He trailed off, the memory of gnawing hunger rising in his gut. He shoved it away and forced himself to finish the story. "I got my claws in her throat. She pulled a mirror out of her pocket and held it up in front of us. Said until the image of hate reflected there changed to one of love, I would never find peace in my animal form. I didn't realize what she was doing until she threw the mirror on the ground. I dived for it, releasing her in the process, and she ported away." He remembered his scream of fury. The shattering of glass as his enemy escaped.

Cyrus drew a notepad out of his pocket, tore off the top page, and handed it to Shim.

He studied the list, a timetable of activities, before staring back in disbelief. "Yoga? Seeking Inner Contentment? *Aromatherapy fucking Massage?* You're messing with me, right?" Waving the list around, he jumped off the bed and started pacing again.

"And you'll spend an hour before dinner with the young weres, helping them with their control lessons. I'll handle the wolves, but I need you to work with Ben. He's a bear so works better on a one-to-one basis. Dana and the cubs need my attention, too." The glare on Rekkus' face at the mention of his mate and new family softened, and envy stabbed Shim's heart.

Fighting his jealousy over the other shifter's joy, he studied the list. "I know I'm going to regret asking this, but what does the P stand for?" The bold letter repeated every morning and afternoon.

"That's from Sarka. She's going to consult our cousin Janessa who has some skills with curse breaking. It will take a few attempts to perfect, but there are some potions she has in mind which may help to reduce your symptoms until the curse can be broken." Cyrus spoke in such a benign voice.

Shim scowled at him. He did not like the idea of being a guinea pig for the eldest Rowan. "And if I don't agree to this regimen?" He knew the answer but just wanted to be sure.

Rekkus pushed away from the wall. "You'll be off the island with my boot up your arse," he snapped, ushering Cyrus out of the room in front of him. The bar thudded down behind them, locking Shim in for the night.

"Someone will be here first thing to let you out. Don't forget you've got Sun Salutations at dawn on the cliffs!" Rekkus' laugh echoed down the corridor, and Shim raised his finger at the closed door.

Fucking yoga....

Chapter Five

C eara hesitated at the door to the dining room, scanning the area with care before she risked entering. A few guests had arrived before her, and they eyed her with interest. Slipping into the room, she took a table in the far corner. The patio doors stood open, and she shivered in the light breeze, but she wanted an exit point available to her.

The wait staff proved discreet and solicitous, bringing her a huge bowl of ripe strawberries, Greek yogurt, and a small pot of honey. An herbal shake and a glass of water were added to the table, and her server left her in peace. She tucked in, having missed her meal in all the turmoil the night before. Her spoon scraped the bottom of the bowl—distracted by the day's activity list, she'd eaten everything.

A waft of jasmine and heather caught her attention. Sage stood next to the table, a sweet smile on her face. The pretty blonde woman carried such an aura of serenity Ceara smiled in response.

Sage held out her hand, and, drawing Ceara's arm through hers, she led her out the door onto the large patio area. "I'm sorry I didn't get to see you last night. Are you well?"

She nodded, allowing Sage to draw her back to

the path she'd followed from her cottage earlier.

"I've been thinking about your problem. I believe the meadow will be a good place for us to begin your therapy." The breeze caught Sage's waist-length hair. She laughed, unhooking her arm to weave her wavy blonde locks into a quick plait. Ceara's own hair lay concealed beneath the knit cap covering her ears. The sun held no warmth for her. Unlike Sage who wore a flowing skirt and thin white blouse, she hid under thick layers of clothing. It made no difference. The cold radiated from deep inside her.

They strolled along the path. Sage set a gentle pace, her light chatter filling in the blanks about the island not covered by Cemil when he'd escorted her to the cottage. Ceara let her mind drift until the mention of some hot springs caught her attention.

Sage smiled. "I thought they might capture your interest. You will have some free time later to explore them. Just keep following the path up past your cottage. It's a hike, but the reward will be worth it."

Reaching a set of intricate wooden gates, Sage swung them open to reveal a carpet of wildflowers and plants, stretching off to the horizon. The sight of bright-yellow blooms froze Ceara in fear, but Sage linked arms with her again, guiding her into the long grass.

"The meadow knows you, will display those plants and flowers most beneficial to you. You will be safe here." The flowers nodded in the breeze as though agreeing with Sage's statement, and Ceara brushed her fingers through the hip-high stems surrounding her.

Sage stood a couple of inches taller than her; the floaty clothing she favored flattered her curves. Ceara's own frame tended toward leanness, although the number of layers she currently wore rounded her out.

Tucking her hand in her pocket, she shivered from cold and memory. "There was faebane," she whispered. "I walked right into a trap, a fire set to draw my team there. To draw me there." The full realization struck her, how the acrid scent of an accelerant disguised the sickly fragrance of the flowers. Someone had set out to harm *her*. Someone with a detailed knowledge of the fae and their weaknesses.

Sage murmured in sympathy, but didn't interrupt, allowing her time to process her thoughts. She already carried the guilt of knowing her friends died because of her failure to control her power. Understanding they'd died because she'd hidden amongst the humans heaped more on her.

"I should never have tried to live in the human world." She sighed. "I told myself working with the rescue squad benefited people, but now I see it was just an excuse to wield my power. I grew too cocky, too sure no one else knew about me. My hubris got them killed." A tear rolled down Ceara's cheek, and Sage reached for her hand and squeezed it.

"From what I understand, you saved a great many lives. Whoever targeted you is to blame. Try to remember that."

They crested a small hill, and Sage paused. The sound of the Wiccan's breath catching in her throat caused Ceara to follow her gaze. A stone circle rose in the distance, a ring of alternate tall and thin and short, wide stones surrounding a huge dolmen in the center.

"One of the things I love about the island is you never know what you will find." Gathering her skirts, Sage ran through the long grass to the circle, Ceara close on her heels.

Stone circles were fae-linked. Some guarded gateways between the realms. Others acted like lodestones, carrying the spirit charge of the humans who worshipped the Lord and Lady. She had visited many of them during her exile, a way of retaining a connection to her own lands. She slipped between a pair of stones, the tall symbolizing male and the shorter female. Energy from the circle rose to greet her, and she sighed in relief. The circle still recognized her as fae, even without her powers. She'd feared the loss of them meant she was mundane. Sage stayed outside the ring, walking a slow circuit. Scattering herbs from the cloth bag over her shoulder, she paced clockwise, whispering a soft invocation.

Ceara approached the dolmen at the center of the circle, and the buzz of energy increased, drawing her closer until she stood beneath the capstone. Stretching her arms out, she could just brush her fingertips against the uprights on either side. The energy tingled against her skin, like sharp pinpricks. She soaked it in, her starved spirit beginning to recharge. Needing to get closer, she stripped down to just a thin tank and shorts. Goose bumps sprang up everywhere, and she pressed herself against the left-hand upright. Power surged over her skin, biting and sharp, but so welcome. The stone grew warm beneath her flesh. Up close she could see the myriad tiny colored crystals hidden within the gray. She turned, resting her back against the stone. Sage raised her arm in a parting wave then wandered through the grass in the direction of the gates.

Deep notches decorated the opposite upright. A fairy ladder. Wedging her fingers and toes into the grooves, Ceara scrambled up the side of the massive stone. Sinews straining, she pulled herself up on top of the capstone. The energy thrummed through the soles of her feet, and she turned in a slow circle to examine the horizon. She expected to be able to see the coastline from her vantage point, but the meadow stretched in every direction, a beautiful carpet of flowers.

She was alone. Sage had vanished from view, the flowers bobbing in the gentle breeze her sole companions. With a sigh of pleasure, she removed the last of her clothing and lay flat on the capstone. The energy from the circle hummed along her skin. Closing her eyes, she let it recharge her broken spirit.

Something tickled against her cheek. She brushed it away, but the sensation remained. Cracking one eye open, she looked for the source. A bud of hope unfurled in her heart when it dawned upon her...she could feel the warmth of the sun on her skin for the first time since the accident.

A rustle in the grass disturbed her. She raised her hand to shield her eyes. The sun shone high overhead now, dazzling her. Sitting up, she faced the noise and frowned at the tall man prowling through the meadow in her direction.

Jet-black hair lay close to his scalp, and his golden-brown skin glowed in the sun. His body flowed with the inborn grace of a shifter, and thick corded muscle packed his shoulders and arms. Dressed in a white T-shirt and cargo shorts, his feet bare, he ate up the distance until he paused at the edge of the circle. The lines feathered around his eyes and two deep grooves etched between his dark brows spoke of age and experience. A scruff of beard graced his jaw and upper lip, flecks of silver glinting in the bright sunshine. His jade eyes gave her the final piece in an unwanted puzzle. *The jaguar*.

Although he remained outside the circle, his presence unnerved her. The hairs on the back of her neck bristled, things long dormant stirring deep in her belly. Rising to her feet, she drew upon every harsh lesson learned at court. Women of the Emerald did not get intimidated by walking beasts—no matter how attractive. *Not possible.*

His gaze traced over her naked form, she fought the urge to preen beneath his attention.

"You were told to stay away from me."

"I was." His deep voice rumbled in his chest, and her nipples pebbled in response.

Words flooded her mind. Primal, base, earthy. Nothing like the preening fools at court nor the softer humans she'd met. Hard, strong, resilient. A man worthy to stand beside the daughter of a queen. His presence prickled over her skin like fireflies dancing in a dusky evening sky.

Taking a step forward, he breached the perimeter of the circle. The energy flowing through her body took on a different resonance. Sharp, fierce power flooded her veins, and she threw her head back, crying out. The world shifted on its axis, the meadow around them altering beyond recognition. The atmosphere thickened, hot and humid with a hint of sulfur. Fronded palms waved in the breeze, choking vines curled around thick trunks, bright tropical flowers spread out before her eyes.

She glanced down, and he stood right there at the foot of the dolmen, his jade eyes glowing. He captured her gaze, held it with ease—not something many men could do—and it ramped up her excitement. He couldn't be called good-looking, in any conventional sense. His features, too scarred and age battered to be considered pretty, were raw, compelling. She wanted nothing more than to leap from her high perch into his embrace.

As though sensing her desire, he took a step back, braced his legs apart, and raised his arms. She swayed on her feet. The energy beneath her pulsed like a heartbeat, strong and steady. Her clit thrummed in time with the flow.

A soft growl rippled around the circle. He drew in a breath and licked his lips. A flush of heat bloomed on her cheeks and throat. Shifters had an amazing sense of smell, and her sudden arousal would be obvious to him. He beckoned impatiently, but she shook her head, fighting his overwhelming presence. Relief vied with disappointment when he retreated, until the moment he paused. Taking three quick steps, he used his powerful leg muscles to spring upward, landing in a crouch at her feet. He crawled across the flat stone, his movements echoing the slinking motion of his hunting cat, until his face pressed into the vee of her thighs.

Intending to push him away, her fingers clutched at his short hair instead. He traced the seam of her pussy with his tongue, a low rumble in his throat vibrating through the tight bundle of nerves. He gripped her ass, pressing her closer to his hot mouth. Yielding to his touch, she allowed him to lift her leg and curl it over his broad shoulder, giving him access to her core. Her knees wobbled when he thrust his tongue deep inside her, licking and probing, taking what he wanted without mercy. Calloused hands tightened their grip, bracing her while he feasted. Staring down at the sight of his head buried between her thighs, she gasped. His short, dark hair glinted in the sun, highlighting the rosette pattern imprinted there. He sucked on her clit, green eyes fixed on hers. She bucked her hips in response to the pull of his lips, and she lost balance. Catching her weight with ease, he lowered her onto her back.

Palming her thighs, he spread them wide before his hungry gaze. "I could scent you from the gates. I couldn't keep away from you."

She lifted on her elbows surprised at the anger in his voice.

"I don't want to be here. Don't want this. Don't

want you," he snarled.

She fought to free her body, but the strength of his hold on her hips increased until she knew bruises would bloom there later.

Eyes glowing in fury and lust, he glared down at her. "What did you do to me? What madness is this? I feel drunk on the taste of you, and I can't get enough." As though to prove his point, he pushed his face back down into her pussy and lapped at her, his tongue gathering the cream flowing from her core.

The hum from the circle, the rasp of his tongue over her clit drove all thoughts of indignation from her head. Sliding back against the hot stone beneath her, she couldn't think, could only ride the lightning of sensation spearing her body. He thrust two thick fingers into her pussy, pumping them in and out at a punishing speed. She gasped and writhed, the noises falling from her mouth guttural and harsh as he fucked her hard with his hand. Teeth clamped around her clit, and he growled, biting down on the sensitive nerves. Her orgasm blasted through her, sending her screaming over the edge of bliss.

A sharp flare of heat ripped through her body. The energy in the circle peaked then settled into a low hum. She whimpered, twisting her hips to try and evade his questing mouth. He snarled, refusing to remove his tongue until he gathered every drop of arousal from her pussy. Sitting back on his heels, Shim wiped his mouth with his hand, pausing to lick his fingers clean before he rose above her.

"I thought your sister was the one to fear." He growled, the glint of anger back in his eyes. "What a fucking idiot I was to believe the Rowans when they told me you were innocent. Everyone knows the fae are tricky bastards, capable of manipulating everyone around them to get what they want."

With a scream of rage, he jumped from the top of

the dolmen, sprinting across the meadow. The steaming jungle had vanished, the meadow once again a mass of summer blooms. Silence lay thick upon the air, sunshine played across her cheek. The soft breeze returned, blowing a strand of her hair over her eyes. Ceara snatched at it in fascination. No longer the dull lifeless brown she'd grown accustomed to since the accident, her hair blazed bright red once again.

Chapter Six

S him ran through the meadow as though the hounds of hell snapped at his heels. His jaguar rode him hard, desperate to turn back to the fae who smelled so good and tasted like heaven on the back of his tongue. The man knew better, though. He'd let Isolde get close enough to capture him because he never looked beyond the surface of her pretty face, and now he'd done worse with Ceara. When he'd caught her smoke-and-spice scent drifting through the gates, he'd been unable to resist its draw. His first instinct had been to find her and apologize in person for his attack, make sure she was unharmed.

Given he'd only seen her bundled up to her ears, the sight of her naked atop the dolmen damn near stopped his heart. Soft brown hair, flowing like melted chocolate over her shoulders and down her back. Her creamy-white skin stretched over lean muscle and ripe curves made his mouth water. But a nice body couldn't explain his instant obsession. She'd shed her disguise, and there had been no mistaking her for anything other than a being with immense power and strength. The stubborn tilt to her chin when she stared down at him, the haughty lift to her brow. The expression in her eyes that said she would take him down, and chew his balls off while she was at it, sent blood rushing to his cock.

And she'd liked him looking at her, regardless of the disdain on her face. When her nipples ripened like berries under his gaze, he'd stopped fighting the attraction. One lick, one taste, and he longed to devour her whole. He knew he hadn't been gentle. The shame of it drove his feet faster. He couldn't condone his rough handling of a female, but she'd driven him beyond sanity. He didn't want to want her. She was the spitting image of Isolde, and yet so different. It confused the hell out of him.

The cat didn't care. He knew by scent and taste she was nothing like her evil sister. Need beat at him, the burning desire to bathe in her body until her essence imprinted on their soul. When she came apart on his tongue, something eased inside him. The cat purred, content they had pleasured her, as was their duty, their right. Shim had been poised, ready to strip off his shorts and bury himself deep inside her wet heat. The shock when he raised his eyes and saw the fiery glow of her hair, the energy pulsing in her eyes had been immense. She had been so clever, playing the victim, luring him in with her body. But she was a liar. If she could alter her appearance with such ease, what else was she capable of?

Shim hit the footpath and slowed his pace, not wishing to draw attention to himself. Rekkus would not be happy he'd disobeyed the instruction to leave the fae alone. He doubted an admission the tiger had been right would assuage his anger at being crossed. He marched along the path to the Haus. He had an appointment with Sarka for another potion to try. The memory of the foul brew she'd forced upon him earlier in the day made him shudder, but he didn't care. He needed this curse broken, and he needed it broken now. The full moon would be in two days, and the jaguar would not be contained during her zenith. Unless he was prepared to suffer a night of agony, he needed to heal his cat, fast.

Shim knocked on the office door, knowing better than to enter before the cool summons. Sarka sat behind the desk, and she beckoned him with an impatient scowl. A brass chalice rested before her on the desk, a dark silk cloth draped over it. Shim eyed it with trepidation. Ice-blue eyes studied him, raising the cat's hackles. He suppressed a hiss. She saw too much. Settling into a seat across from her, he regretted not taking the time to collect himself better before facing her.

"You look agitated, Shimeer. If you no longer require my assistance, you need only to say so." Her icy glare spread to her voice. Closing his eyes, he sucked in a cleansing breath. The sharp edge of her scent swirled around the room. The anger in it was abstract, not aimed at him. A long-simmering tension she carried with her. If a man had caused such rage, he felt damn sorry for the bastard. He lifted his lids, the cat inside him curious about the enigmatic woman opposite.

Sarka removed the cloth from the chalice, and, with a nasty grin, slid the cup over the desk. "You didn't have quite the reaction I'd hoped to the potion I gave you this morning. I've chatted with Janessa, and we think this combination might be more successful." His curiosity fled. He knew everything about the Wiccan he needed.

The contents of the chalice sloshed, the viscous brew clinging to the sides of the cup before settling again. Green and brackish, it reminded him of a pool of stagnant water. He'd drunk from such a pool when a young cub and been sick for days afterwards. Not an experience he was keen to repeat any time soon.

She drummed her fingers on the arm of her

chair, and he sighed, reaching for the cup. The acrid scent brought tears to his eyes. Squeezing them shut, he threw the entire contents down his throat. His stomach rebelled at the foul taste, and he clamped a hand tight over his mouth to avoid spewing the brew onto the desk. His jaguar whined and fled to the far reaches of his consciousness, seeking to distance himself from the evil liquid coating his tongue and throat. It chased away the lingering taste of Ceara in his mouth, which he should have been grateful for, but it left him bereft.

Opening his eyes once he'd convinced his stomach its contents would have to stay, he scowled at the look of delight wreathing Sarka's face before she dropped her mask of indifference back into place.

"So, how was that?" she asked in a sweet tone that didn't suit her. He suspected these sessions were more punishment than cure.

He cleared his throat, swallowing to force the last of the thick liquid down before he spoke. "Not bad."

She snorted once, reaching for a leather-bound book to make notes. Her dark hair fell around her face, creating a curtain. She carried on writing, ignoring him until the tension in the room stretched his nerves to the screaming point.

"Better check your schedule," she said without lifting her head. "You've got a breathing and meditation class with Trixie in a couple of minutes."

He snarled and threw himself out of the chair, stomping to the door. He froze at the soft snicker rising behind him. Storming out of the room, he banged straight into Rekkus. The were-tiger took one sniff and scowled.

"You have got to be freaking kidding me. I told you to stay away from her," he snarled.

"Don't start with me, Rekkus, I'm not in the mood," Shim snapped back. "I won't be going near that hateful little bitch again, so you have nothing to worry about. Wait until you see her. She's played you all for fools with her 'poor little me' act."

He stepped around Rekkus, heading down the corridor leading to the meditation suite. The big man blocked his path, grabbed his shoulder in a tight grip, and forced him to halt.

"Hateful, is she?" A purr hinted in his voice.

Shim snapped his eyes up to meet the thoughtful golden gaze.

"I know we are different breeds, jaguar, but your cat is pretty similar to mine in most things. If you hate the fae so much, ask yourself why you carry her scent on your skin still." Rekkus released his shoulder, folding his arms across his thick chest. "I need you down at the training fields in about an hour. Telly and the other wolves are a handful, and I can't give them and Ben the attention they all need. The bear cub needs some one-on-one time. Make sure you have a goddamn wash before you show up. You reek of sex, and that's the last thing those boys need to scent."

Shim toweled off his short hair and pulled clean clothes from his duffle. The contents of his room in the main Haus had been transferred. He would be sleeping in the barracks until Rekkus told him otherwise. Gathering his dirty clothes, he paused. The T-shirt still carried Ceara's heat and spice. He shoved it under his pillow, refusing to examine his motivation for doing so. He donned a fresh shirt and pants. He would be going to dinner after his session with Ben, so he might as well be ready.

The kid sat on his bed, reading a book, when Shim knocked on the doorframe, startling him a little. He stayed outside the room, not wanting to crowd the boy by invading his territory. Ben might be only fifteen, but the boy matched him in height. He was broader, too, although a lot less graceful. The sweet-natured young man was diffident, a little too conscious of his size. Had he hurt someone by accident, or was he struggling to adjust to a recent growth spurt?

"Hey, Ben. I want to stretch my legs and thought maybe you would like to join me." The naked delight on the boy's face eased the stress inside Shim. Pushing thoughts of Ceara out of his mind, he concentrated on his task. The diminishment of his own prowl robbed him of the chance to mentor young shifters. They strolled away from the barracks in companionable silence, wending their way to the training fields. Steering his charge around the perimeter, Shim gave the young man a chance to settle himself in the presence of a very dominant elder.

"Have you been to the island before, Ben?" He kept his voice quiet, and the young cub nodded but didn't speak. Smiling to himself, he tried again. "Well, you will know the area better than I do, then. Why don't you show me your favorite spot?"

Ben glanced sideways at Shim, and, after receiving a nod of encouragement, took the lead, heading away from the fields toward the river which ran close by. Trees and large boulders lined the banks. Ben selected a square, flat-topped stone, clambering on top with an agility belying his size. Shim leapt up, trying not to think about the dolmen in the middle of the stone circle. He settled cross-legged on the boulder, facing the water. Ben took off his shoes, letting his feet dangle over the edge so they hung above the slow-moving river. The boy had chosen a peaceful spot, quiet except for the rippling water and the odd splash of a fish breaking the surface. Excited barks from the little wolf pack carried on the breeze as Rekkus put the other boys through their paces far away on the training field.

Shim cast his mind back to a long time ago, remembering the excitement and uncertainty of being on the cusp of adulthood. The pull of the moon like a siren he couldn't ignore, bringing uncontrollable changes and the urge to rut on anything remotely female. There'd been more than one embarrassing encounter when he'd come across the girls from the local village bathing and playing in the stream. He shook his head, recalling the hours spent lurking in the trees in his jaguar form, spying on them.

"I was a goddamn Peeping Tom at your age, Ben." He laughed, explaining a little about his youthful misadventures. The young bear relaxed and laughed along with him before growing contemplative as he stared out across the river.

"How do you know when you've met your mate? I asked Rekkus, but he just grunted and said I would know. I'm so confused." A faint blush highlighted Ben's freckled cheeks. He kept his face turned away, so Shim could only study his profile.

The question caught him by surprise, and he gave his answer careful consideration. "My father told me from the moment he first caught my mother's scent, he was captivated by her. Trailed her for days through the jungle, lurking on the edge of her family's territory too scared to approach her. Mama said she knew he was there, but she refused to acknowledge him, wanting to see if he would make an effort to win her over. When the full moon struck, he cried all night for her until her father lost his temper and chased him away." Shim smiled at the memory of the affectionate teasing between his parents when they'd first told him the story.

"He kept coming back, and Papi kept chasing him off, but my father said he could never give up without claiming her." His jaguar surged, snarling and rubbing close beneath his skin, catching him off guard. Smoke-and-spice curled through his mind, and he recalled Rekkus' comment about Shim being bathed in Ceara's scent.

Oh shit!

The realization hit like a ton of bricks. He clenched his fists, fighting to keep in control. The jaguar strained against his hold, impatient it had taken the man so long to catch up with what he'd known from the first moment he'd buried his nose in her creamy throat.

Ceara was his mate. The perfect half the Fates decreed would make him whole. And he'd tried to kill her at their first meeting then almost forced himself upon her at their second.

"Shim, is everything all right, sir?" The diffident tone from the boy brought him back to himself.

He cut his growl off, forcing himself to relax. His palms stung. His claws had come out, piercing bloody wounds where he'd balled his fists. "I'm fine, Ben. I've been an idiot about a few things, and my cat is a little irritated with me because of it. You're too young to be worried about mating, but I would say trust your instincts and, when the time is right, you'll know."

"There's a girl I like at school. She smells like sunshine and clover. She makes my head spin, and I say dumb stuff to her all the time." Ben sighed. Reaching for a small stone, he skimmed it across the surface of the river. "She's not a bear, though. She's just a human, and my mama says she won't understand how it is for us weres if I try and tell her how I feel." The boy sounded so despondent, Shim swallowed a laugh.

"I remember a time when all girls smelled like heaven, Ben. Just because you are attracted to her, doesn't mean she is your mate. I fell in and out of love with every girl in the local village over a period of about four years, so maybe cut yourself some slack and just see what happens."

The young man nodded. "She has a friend who smells like strawberries. I like strawberries."

Shim laughed and clapped Ben on the shoulder before pulling him to his feet. The sun had crossed the sky during their talk. He needed to get the boy back to the security of the barracks before night fell and the moon called forth his bear.

And then he had some serious mate claiming to do.

Chapter Seven

C eara smoothed her hand over the white silk dress she unearthed from the bottom of her suitcase. The energy from the circle still sang in her veins. A fruitless hour spent in front of the hearth, trying and failing to coax the flames to respond, had led to a flurry of bitter tears. The boost from the circle had driven the worst of the cold away. Her righteous fury at the damned cat helped to warm her further. The mere thought of him brought a flood of dampness between her legs. So humiliating! He was little better than an animal and arrogant with it. She was a daughter of the Unseelie Court, an immortal fae. Not some damn plaything for him to pick up and drop whenever he felt like it.

With a sigh, she met her reflection in the bathroom mirror. Too old to lie to herself, the truth struck deep. Shim had played her body better than any other male then rejected her. It hurt her pride, maybe her heart just a little bit. Hence the outfit. A good dress served better than a suit of armor— another hard-won lesson of court. Rumpling her hair until it cascaded down her back like fire, she retouched the matching red lipstick coating her mouth, emphasizing her full lower lip. Her feet remained bare, touching the earth would help to keep her grounded.

The dining room hummed with activity by the time she arrived. She didn't hesitate, crossing into the darker-green side of the room. She was not mundane. Not human. No more hiding. A hush followed her progress, and she raised her chin. *Let them look.*

A chair scraped back, the harsh noise drawing her attention. The jaguar stood, looking damn fine in his dark-green shirt and black evening slacks. He gestured to the seat opposite him. She curled her lip in a sneer of disbelief at his arrogance. Choosing an unoccupied table, she stood beside a chair, waiting for one of the waiters to pull it out for her. She'd barely settled before he approached, taking the seat next to her as though he had every right to do so. Determined to ignore him, she turned to the waiter with a gracious smile, accepting the offered menu. He poured a glass of ice water, bowed, and withdrew to a discreet distance.

Shim lounged back in his chair, his body language relaxed. He summoned the waiter to transfer his drink and silverware across to his new seat. "I'll be taking my meal with the Lady Ceara this evening."

She let out a jagged laugh. "Lady is it now? You've changed your tune, *cat.*" She hissed the last word at him. Her palm itched with the desire to slap the smile off his rugged, handsome features. Wait! That wasn't what she thought when she looked at him. *It wasn't!*

She reached for her glass of water, not sure whether she should throw it in his face or dump it over her head to quench the desire churning low in her belly. As though sensing her intentions, Shim grasped her hand and captured it in his own. He massaged the palm of her hand with the ball of his thumb. His touch rocketed through her body, making her fight against the urge to squirm in her seat. Keeping his jade-green eyes fixed on hers, he drew her arm closer, turning her wrist to bare the pale, almost translucent skin. He lowered his face, pressing his nose against her skin, and drew in a breath. A deep rumbling sound built in his chest, and she blinked at him in astonishment.

Is he actually purring?

His wicked tongue stroked over her pulse point, and she couldn't fight a shudder. The wet heat conjured images of him kneeling between her thighs.

Biting hard on the inside of her cheek, she used the small pain to focus her thoughts. She yanked her hand free, tucking it in her lap. Resting his elbows on the table, he placed his chin on his folded hands, studying her.

"I'm sorry, *mi tesoro*." He pitched his husky voice low, for her ears alone, and Ceara frowned at the unexpected endearment. His behavior seemed so at odds with his angry departure from the meadow. She didn't know what to make of it.

"What exactly are you sorry for?" she muttered. "Are you sorry you tried to kill me? Sorry you insulted me? Sorry you made me come with your mouth?"

A well of anger had been building since their encounter, replacing the numbness of her existence. She wanted to scream, wanted to lash out, to scour the world with fire and vengeance until she found the person responsible for the deaths of her team. She glared at him, and, for a second, she hated him. He'd shocked her out of her lethargy, forced her to feel again. Hadn't even had the decency to put her out of her misery when he'd had the chance.

The anger boiled, a living thing crawling in her gut. Wetting her lips, she slicked moisture over the shimmer of red lipstick. His body language shifted, keen and sharp. He bent his entire focus upon her, and she shuddered. Opening her mouth to speak, she froze when the waiter appeared with their food. After an imperceptible shake of his head in her direction, Shim smiled and thanked the waiter. He raised his silverware and cut a thick slice of the rare steak in front of him. Tilting his head toward her plate, he lifted the piece of meat to his mouth.

"You need to eat, *querida*. You look magnificent in your fury, and it's such a turn-on, but if we're going to have a proper fight, then you need to keep your strength up." He chewed the steak, cut another slice before placing his knife and fork down. "Eat, Ceara." This time it wasn't a request, and she couldn't help but respond to the dominance in his command.

She ate mechanically—cut, bite, chew, swallow, repeat. The last vestige of rationality in her mind said the food tasted delicious, had been prepared to perfection. It might have been a fast food burger for all the attention she paid to it. He ate fast, his efficient movements clearing his plate well before she finished, although he'd started with a much larger portion. Handing her the glass of water, he watched her raise it to her mouth. She drained the contents until he nodded in satisfaction. Rising from his chair, he prowled around the small table to stand at her back. He eased the seat as she stood then captured her hand. Placing it on his forearm in a courtly gesture, he escorted her from the dining room. Rage boiled so close to the surface, her entire body vibrated with the tension of it.

Leaning close, he pressed his mouth to her ear. "Hold on to it for just a little bit longer." He bit down on the tender lobe, a sharp sting, followed by a soothing lick. She stiffened her posture to avoid arching her back, pleasure racing through her. Passing the reception desk, he smiled at Myron.

The young woman grabbed her deck of cards and dealt five out on the desk before she laughed. "You are in so much trouble, kitty."

Shrugging as though it were no big deal, he continued to lead Ceara outside.

The moment they cleared the light shining through the entranceway, he quickened his pace, dragging her into a stand of trees just off the pathway. She yanked her hand away, her action so violent she staggered a little before rounding on him. He towered over her by at least a foot, and she stretched up on tiptoes to deliver a hard slap to his cheek. The blow knocked his lip against his teeth, and he grinned, licking the spot of blood from his mouth.

"Feel better, *querida*?" he taunted.

She launched herself at him, a flurry of fists and teeth, striking him over and over. Standing firm, he let her vent her frustration against him. Her hands hurt from pounding against his thick chest, his solid thighs and arms, but she couldn't stop. All the pain and sorrow she'd buried came flooding to the surface. Tears burned behind her eyes, but she refused to let them free. She didn't want to mourn, she wanted the rage, needed it to keep her heart protected.

Shim grabbed her by the waist. Over-balancing Ceara, he took them both to the ground, rolling in a fluid motion so he landed flat on his back with her sprawled over him. She clawed at his shirt, ripping the buttons free to find his flesh. Nails digging deep, she marked his golden skin. He let out a moan, lifting his knees so she slid down to straddle his lap. The thick length of his cock rubbed against her pussy through the thin silk of her dress. Incapable of rational thought, she crawled up his body to clamp her mouth over his.

She bit his lower lip hard, and he rumbled in approval, the vibration in his chest teasing against her nipples. He gripped her chin, forced her mouth to open, and plunged his tongue deep. Palming her ass, he pressed the juncture of her thighs down, thrusting his hips against her.

Tearing her mouth away, she scored his chest, threw her head back, and screamed. The fat disc of the burgeoning moon shone through the tops of the trees, the symbol of the goddess watching over them both. She ground her hips, rubbing desperately against the seam of his pants. It wasn't enough. She needed to be closer. Needed skin against skin. Lifting off, she fumbled with his belt buckle.

Shim grabbed her hand. Stilling her movements, he panted for breath. "Not here, *flamita*. We are too close to the Haus and someone might disturb us. Where are you staying? I didn't scent you on the second floor. Not with the human guests?"

"They gave me a cottage. It's near the meadow." Her voice sounded husky and unfamiliar to her ears. He had successfully transmuted her anger to lust, and she wanted nothing more than to ride this man to oblivion. She rubbed against his hips again, and he growled, smacking her ass. Rolling to his feet in one graceful move, he threw her over his shoulder.

The indignity of it would not be borne. "Put me down, you beast!" Ceara yelled.

Sharp teeth sank into the rounded flesh of her ass. She yelped in shock, and his palm cracked across the other cheek before he flowed into action. He ran like silk, like water flowing over rocks. His feet ate up the ground, giving her no choice but to grab the back of his belt and hold on for the ride. They reached the gates of the meadow before she knew it, and he paused. Ceara shoved her hair out of her face, pointed up the hill, and he moved again.

Shifting to the left, he dove into the tree line, finding the little path to the cottage without her saying anything, no doubt following her scent trail. Slamming the door of the cottage open, he lowered her onto her feet, stepping back to leave a modicum of space between their bodies.

His chest rose and fell in a lazy action, jade eyes glittering in the firelight. She'd banked the fireplace before she'd left. The inside of the cottage remained warm, the soft glow from the flames lit the room. He studied her, his intense look sending shivers down her spine. Whatever courage, or madness, had caused her brazen actions in the trees had fled somewhere during the journey. Ducking her head away from his eyes, she glanced at his chest, his powerful physique visible through the tattered remains of his shirt. Thick scratches gouged his skin, and she raised her hands in front of her, shocked at the sight of blood beneath her nails. She flicked her eyes up, blinking in astonishment at the look of pleasure on his face.

"I like your marks on me, *querida*." He growled, tugging the remains of his shirt free. Slabs of muscle cut down his abdomen, a clear line defining each side arrowing down to his hips. She licked her dry lips, wanting to trace the indent with her tongue, to chase it lower and lower until she reached the prize she knew awaited her.

He loosened his belt and unzipped his slacks. The dark material slid to the floor, revealing soft cotton boxer briefs stretched over his cock like a second skin. Stepping forward, she grasped the waistband. Sliding them down his thighs, she dropped to her knees. His rigid flesh sprang free, slapping against his lower belly. She moaned, reaching greedily with both hands. He grunted as she guided the head of his cock between her lips. Gathering her hair in a tight grip, he pulled it back into a long tail, wrapping the strands around his fist.

She hummed in pleasure at the sting across her

scalp when he pulled her hair. Bobbing her head, she sucked more of his length into her mouth. Playing her tongue along the underside, she probed with the tip into the sensitive spot just beneath his head. Shim growled, bucking his hips. Nudging his thighs apart, she slipped her hand lower to cup his balls, stretching her lips wider to draw the last few inches into her mouth. The taste of him on her tongue, rich and heady with a hint of eucalyptus and spicy cloves, sent her desire into orbit. Moisture pooled between her thighs. Hard hands tugged on her hair again and she saw stars.

She rolled her eyes up to meet his; the jade green glittered in the firelight. She hollowed her cheeks, sucking hard on his cock, and his eyes blazed. Withdrawing her mouth in slow increments, she stopped when just the head remained between her lips. She swirled her tongue, holding his gaze, teasing the slit. He pulled her head with a sharp jerk of her hair, and she released her prize with an audible pop. Sweat glistened on his chest. Holding her still, he drew a couple of shuddering breaths. The grip in her hair loosened, and he reached beneath her arms, lifting her to her feet. His hands skimmed her arms, petting and stroking until they met at the neck of her dress. A sharp noise filled the air as he tugged his hands apart, rending the silk in two. The ruined material slid from her shoulders, leaving her naked except for a wisp of matching silk at her hips.

"Mine," he growled.

Chapter Eight

Saliva pooled in his mouth at the sight of his perfect little mate almost bared to him. He hooked his fingers into the sides of her underwear and flicked a claw, shredding the material so it fell to the floor at her feet. The soft red curls at the juncture of her thighs glistened with evidence of her arousal. He trailed his thumbs across the jut of her hip bones that framed the feminine curve of her belly. Muscles twitched beneath his hand. He skimmed lower, delighting in every shudder. Parting her labia, he knelt before her, bent his head, and thrust his tongue between her lips. Her unique smoke-and-spice flavor burst in his mouth.

He wrapped his lips around her clit, growling hard, knowing the sensation would drive her crazy. She moaned and squirmed away from him, which didn't please Shim or his cat. Wary, he tracked her movements, stalking her every step on his hands and knees. His little fae spun away, fleeing toward the back of the open-plan room. She ducked behind a thin curtain, vanishing from sight.

Shim roared and lunged through the gauzy material, pulling up at the arresting sight. His mate posed on her hands and knees in the center of a huge bed, flame-red hair spilling everywhere. She peered at him over her shoulder, a wicked smile curling her lips.

He fisted his cock and, squeezing the base, he sought a modicum of control. His mate licked her lips then lowered her face to the bed covers. The motion caused her hips to undulate and she parted her legs, displaying her pussy to his greedy eyes. He climbed behind her, the bed shifting beneath his weight. Tracing his fingertips up the backs of her calves and thighs, he locked them on her hips. She sighed, relaxing into his firm grip. Shim lined his cock up at her entrance, thrusting balls deep in a single stroke. Heaven, right there in her slick, hot channel. He fought to hold still, giving her a chance to adapt to his thickness. His muscles twitched with his desire to pull back and thrust again, but her tight sex clenched, squeezing his cock until his eyes rolled back in his head.

"Move, Shim! For the love of the Lord and Lady, fuck me!"

Helpless to do anything else, he obeyed her demands. Withdrawing almost his entire length, he slammed his hips forward, pistoning in and out of her pussy without relenting. Sights and scents sharpened, the jaguar rising within him. The increased stimuli set his brain on fire. His mate braced her head on her arms, lifting her body in an act of the sweetest surrender. The pressure in his balls increased with each thrust, until they drew up tight. He shifted his hips, blanketing his body over her back, fighting the urge to flood her sweet pussy with his seed.

Sweat drenched them both, their slick bodies slipping and sliding together. Shortening his thrusts, he curled an arm around her slender waist, delving between her legs. He captured her clit between his seeking fingers, pinching hard. The sheets muffled her cries of passion. He tweaked the bundle of nerves in time with the motion of his hips, and her pussy clamped down on his cock like a band of molten steel.

A deep roar ripped from his throat. Her wild release milked his own. He relished the burn of his seed filling his mate, coating her in his scent, marking her his forever. The siren call of the full moon rippled through him, and Shim threw his soul wide open as the mating bond snapped into place.

His strength gave out, and he fell sideways, twisting his hips so she landed on top, not wanting to crush her with his weight. Her sweat-dampened hair draped over his face, but he didn't have the strength to brush it away. Chest heaving, he sucked in oxygen, reveling in the new connection to his mate.

"I'm still mad at you." She panted, although made no move to separate their bodies.

Shim chuckled, tracing a finger down her side, loving the shiver of goose bumps rising to greet his touch.

"Give me a minute to recover, and we can start that fight again, *mi tesoro.*"

The spicy scent of ginger and peppercorns tickled his nose. He cracked an eyelid, squeezing it closed at the bright sunshine flooding through the window above the bed. Water pattered against tile before shutting off. Forcing himself to his elbows, he watched the bathroom door swing open and Ceara appeared in a cloud of scented steam, body and hair wrapped in matching dark-green towels.

She rubbed a spot on her shoulder. He grinned to himself, knowing she traced the mark he'd placed on her skin during their second coupling. A matching one rode high on her hip, a trophy from the third time he took her. His jaguar stirred, the cat still drunk on the scent and sensation of claiming their mate. She intoxicated him, and he wanted nothing more than to pull her back into bed with him.

"Good morning, *querida*." He purred, patting the empty side of the bed next to him.

"Good morning, Shimeer." Her voice sounded haughty, a little cool, and he held back a snarl of displeasure.

The cream cotton sheets knotted about his legs, thwarting his efforts to grab her when she skirted the bed. Keeping her back to him, she pulled clothing from the chest of drawers tucked away in the corner. Wrestling free, he flung back the sheet, pausing on the edge of the bed when she turned to face him. A faint blush stained her throat and the top of her chest. His erection stiffened further under her stare. Stroking his flesh, he contemplated all the ways he wanted to play with his mate. Regardless of her icy tone and stiff posture, his woman's scent told a different story. A day in bed would soon have his little spitfire sinking her nails into him.

"There's some tea if you want it." Her voice brisk, she tugged on plain cotton shorts and a matching tank-style bra. He growled, hating the material shielding more of her delectable skin.

"Come back to bed, *flamita*. I have lots of plans for you, and none of them involve you wearing any clothing."

Ignoring him, she pulled on a pair of stretchy yoga pants to match the navy, long-sleeve top she already wore. The material covered his marks on her skin. He snarled, wanting them on show. While shifters would recognize his scent claim the instant they came into contact with Ceara, his bite would act as a visible display, warning other paras to keep their distance, too.

She is my mate and should be proud to display them.

"I've got an appointment this morning. Sage has arranged for me to meet with one of the other healers, and I'm willing to try anything at this point."

He sighed to demonstrate his aggravation at being thwarted by practicalities. Romping with his beautiful little fae would have to take a backseat for the moment. Her healing was of paramount importance to him. He wanted her fit and whole, and it was also time to focus on his own problems. Not being able to use his jaguar form to protect her was unacceptable. He would swallow any number of noxious potions, suffer the indignities of "downward-facing dog" if the Rowans believed it would break him free of the curse.

His jaguar grew increasingly restless, the tug of the full moon making it worse. He jumped from the bed and headed for the shower. At least he could use his mate's soaps and carry the scent with him while they were apart.

"I thought we could take a walk later. I've heard great things about the hot springs if you—" He stopped scrubbing his hair with a towel. He spoke to an empty room. His sneaky little mate had escaped in the few minutes it took him to use the bathroom. Her absence settled along his skin like the ashes coating the fireplace.

He dressed, taking the time to clean out the hearth and build a new fire ready to be lit on her return. The needs of his mate came first, but if she thought she could evade him for long, she would be sorely disappointed. Shim might not be able to hold his shift, but he retained every single one of his predatory instincts, and he was on the hunt. He'd successfully claimed Ceara's body, now to fight for her heart.

Myron greeted Shim with a broad grin and a wink, pausing in her conversation with Cyrus. The dark-haired Wiccan looked relaxed, bantering back and forth with the receptionist. Did the nature of their relationship extend beyond employer and employee?

Rekkus stepped out of the office behind reception. His attention swiveled straight to him. Moving with imperceptible swiftness, he glided from behind the desk to place himself between Shim and Cyrus. He might be head of security on the island, but first and foremost he served as Cyrus' bodyguard. A flare of nostrils and a single blink were the only tells Rekkus gave to acknowledge Shim's altered scent. He leaned into Cyrus to whisper something. The Wiccan removed the mirrored glasses from his face. Tilting his dark head to one side, he studied Shim with piercing blue eyes, identical to his sister's.

"Fascinating. Do you feel any different?" An undercurrent of excitement laced the man's voice, and Shim grasped at it like a lifeline.

Could it be so simple? Was his mating the key to breaking the curse? Clad only in a T-shirt and sweatpants, it took moments to shed his clothing. He'd changed in his room in the barracks before heading to the main Haus. He had nothing to hide about his activities of the previous night, but Ceara might not appreciate the rumors it would cause if he did a walk of shame in the same clothing he'd worn to dinner. Especially if she was under the misapprehension theirs was a casual fling.

Myron whistled, clapping her hands together. "One of the great things about this job is the amount of fine ass I get to see," she exclaimed.

Rekkus snarled, grabbed his arm, and shoved him into a room behind reception, Cyrus on their heels.

"Not in front of the humans, dammit! It took all of Cemil's considerable powers of persuasion to get them to swallow our explanation after your stunt in the bloody dining room."

"You spoil all my fun," Myron pouted.

Cyrus shook his head and closed the door in her face.

Too close to prevent his shift, Shim dropped onto all fours, calling forth his jaguar. The familiar snap and twist of bone and sinew—a pain he would always welcome—and his body shifted to his animal form. Nails elongated to claws; black fur rippled over his skin, washing down his spine. His tail sprang forth. Bracing the pads of his thick paws on the cool tile floor, he flexed his claws, shaking out the last aches of his shift. His jaguar chuffed at Rekkus, the tiger's strong musk an irritant in such close quarters. The big man curled a lip and gave him the finger.

Cyrus crouched before him, tapping a finger under his powerful jaws. He lifted his head higher, permitting the Wiccan to examine his eyes. For a few blissful moments, he embraced the unity with his other self, thanking the Fates for delivering his mate and ending his suffering.

A slow burn, a familiar and dreaded itch, started between his shoulder blades. He rolled his neck, not wanting to acknowledge it. The man before him blurred, a ripple of agony danced along his spine, and the curse struck. Roaring in despair, he forced the jaguar down and resumed his human form. The pain continued to prickle along skin always sensitive post-shift, and he flinched away before the man could touch him.

A square of white cloth dangled before his streaming eyes. He reached for it, blowing his noise, wiping his cheeks. "That's a no, then."

He shrugged, trying to make light of the

situation, ignoring the raging fear inside. He would find a way to break the curse. Struggling into his clothing, he appreciated their discretion when the two men averted their eyes. His nudity didn't bother him. Shifters didn't think twice about stripping before each other. He knew they were giving him space to adjust to the disappointment of still being at the mercy of his curse.

"Have you completed the mating?" Rekkus asked.

He shook his weary head in response. "I think Ceara needs a little more time to come to terms with parts of our relationship."

Rekkus snorted. "Which parts, exactly?"

Shim gave him a rueful grin. "The *relationship* part."

He sighed, enduring the loud burst of laughter from both men as they left the room. The noise drew a glaring Sarka out of her office, and she clicked her fingers in an imperious gesture at Shim.

"Time for your potion, snot boy, and this one is gonna be a doozy."

Just when I thought things couldn't get any worse.

Chapter Nine

Sage left after introducing Ceara to a small wizened man. Add a red pointy hat and a beard and he would be the perfect image of the ceramic garden gnomes humans loved to decorate their gardens with. He shook her hand, his skin surprisingly soft for all its wrinkles and liver spots.

"A pleasure to meet you, my dear. My name is Robert, and I am honored to assist a Shining One. Lie back on the table and we'll get started." She hesitated, and he gave her a kind smile. "If it makes you more comfortable, you can leave your clothing on. I don't need to touch you to carry out my psychic scan."

Settling back, she tried to relax. Soft music and the sounds of a rippling stream filled the room.

"Close your eyes, my dear. Just listen to the music and try to forget I am here." Robert's kind voice matched the twinkle in his gray eyes, and she did as he bade.

An image from the previous night rose in her mind's eye. Shim leaning over her, rocking tenderly into her body. Their first fierce coupling melting into delicate intimacies and moments of sheer bliss. She'd cried at the unbearable perfection, and she remembered the soft press of his mouth when he kissed the tears from her cheek. She'd fallen asleep cocooned in his warm embrace, the drape of his body over hers so good, so right. For the first time since the accident, the chill had been banished from her body.

Soft snores woke her just after dawn. She'd lain there for a moment, relishing their closeness. Letting herself drift and daydream, she imagined waking beside him every morning. Instead of dread, calmness took root deep within her.

But then the wash of guilt knocked the wind out of her—she had no right to happiness in the wake of causing so much death and destruction. The wives and girlfriends of the men on her team would never again sleep in the comfort of their embrace. Their children would never feel the soft brush of Daddy's kiss on their forehead. Self-loathing forced her from the warmth and comfort of the bed and into the shower. The confusion on his face when she avoided his touch became another layer of guilt. He'd taken everything she threw at him, let her vent her anger and pain on his flesh, without complaint or censure.

The endless loop of her thoughts threatened to drive her insane. Pushing back the memories, she drew a breath and held it for a count of five before releasing it for the same count, using the breathing exercises she'd learned in Trixie's classes. The willowy fae had been kind, if a little wary of Ceara, a natural reaction from one of the Seelie Court raised to believe every Unseelie was the monster lurking under their bed. In Ceara's case, the monster was one of her uncles by marriage, although he'd cut down on his child snatching since her aunt disapproved of it.

The deep breathing helped, and Robert surprised her with a very light pat on her arm as he told her to sit up. He turned the background music down low, rolling a stool over to the side of the couch so he could sit close without invading her personal space.

"Well, my dear, I think I see the problem. There is evidence of a catastrophic injury to your soul, of a magnitude unlike any I have seen before. It's a miracle you are still able to function." The old man's eyes shone with sympathy, and she rubbed her chest in reflex.

"The good news is there is also some evidence of healing. The best way I can describe what I 'see' is a huge bruise. The edges have started to fade. I expect the mating bond will further improve the damage."

Ceara raised her hand to interrupt him, "Mating bond?" Her voice rasped, and she cleared her throat before trying again. "What mating bond?" A faint tremor started in her arm, and she couldn't control it. Her hand shook so hard she tucked it under her other arm to hide it. Random synapses firing in her brain, she tried to process what the psychic meant.

A look of alarm creased the old man's face. "Oh! Oh my dear girl, I assumed you knew! The bond looks new made to me. I don't have a great deal of experience with them, but Rekkus' mate, Dana, has been kind enough to let me study their bond a few times."

A gentle tug freed her hand from beneath her armpit, and he curled her fingers around a large glass of water. Holding it steady, he encouraged her to take a few sips. The shock of cold sliding down her throat roused her sufficiently, and she gripped the smooth surface, taking another drink. Nodding her thanks for his assistance, she drained the water. Robert retreated to his stool, rolling away and giving his patient a little more space.

"I understand you have suffered a shock, my dear. I must apologize again for my crass insensitivity. But if you will indulge an old man, then I would say this mating may be just what you need to heal. At the moment, the link is tentative. Your mate will always be connected to you, but the bond won't flourish until you complete the ceremony and share your soul with him."

Ceara rolled the cold glass over her forehead, trying to gather her scattered wits. Shim had mated with her. *How the hell did we go from mortal enemies, to lovers, to potential mates in such a short space of time?* The bloody Fates must be laughing their asses off.

She thought about the prophecy and shuddered. Maybe Isolde had been right, apart from assuming she was the one frozen, and not Ceara. Prophecies tended to be spouted by lunatics, their fevered brains touched by the Lord and Lady. You could never rely on them making sense. The gods loved to put a sting in the tale. And the queen knew her location, would be looking for her when she left the island.

She placed her empty glass on the couch and rubbed her face. "I don't want this." Tears trickled down her cheeks. A soft hand rested on the top of her head, and Robert stroked her hair.

"Poor girl, you must forgive yourself for what happened. Your loss of control was not a deliberate act. Sage explained to me about the presence of the faebane. In my opinion, the damage to your soul is self-imposed. Would your friends want you to suffer so? Whoever laid the trap for you will win if you let them ruin the rest of your life." He pressed a tissue into her shaky grasp then crossed the room. Busying himself at the little sink, he rinsed and dried her empty glass.

Wiping her eyes, she slipped down from the couch and moved to the door. She paused, fingers curled around the handle when Robert murmured, "Speak to your mate, my dear. Give him a chance to explain. And remember, the Fates gifted you this precious connection for a reason."

Ceara gave a mirthless laugh. He had such a romantic soul and far more faith in the Fates than she did. "You see a gift. But I fear this bond will deliver our doom. Happy ever after is for fairy tales, Robert, and I am not a fairy. I am fae. Unseelie fae."

Wanting to avoid the reception area, she slipped instead out a side door. Needing some peace and quiet to contemplate her next move, she followed the winding path along the cliffs behind the Haus. The ever-present fog bank lurked just offshore, ringing the island. The heat from the sun seemed powerless to burn back the haze. Rounding the corner, she pulled up at the sight of a yoga class spread out across the grassy area overlooking the bright-blue sea. A mixed group, the majority humans, with a couple of paras spread through them. Including her mate. An incongruous sight—Shim braced on all fours with his fine, firm ass sticking up in the air.

A couple of human women were positioned behind him, and she didn't appreciate them paying more attention to her lover's ass than their own posture. A wave of jealousy, black and strong, swept through Ceara. She reached for her fire without conscious thought. Emptiness echoed in her soul, but the flash of emotion proved strong enough to capture her mate's attention. He flowed from his yoga stance to his feet.

Caring and concern glowing bright in his eyes, he wove through the group. Such a glorious sight, strength and surety in every move of his delicious body. Few would consider him handsome, but his rugged, hard face appealed to her. Used by life. The kind of partner who could be relied upon, given the opportunity. He paused less than a foot away; the heat radiating off his body called to her like a beacon.

"You mated me." The calmness of her voice

surprised her.

A snicker of laughter came from behind them, where the two human women sat cross-legged on their mats, watching them avidly.

"These two are the gift that keeps on giving," the brunette said to her friend, and they giggled again.

Shim growled, capturing her attention, and the humans were forgotten.

"You mated me," she repeated, and he nodded once.

"I did. Don't ask me to apologize, *flamita,* because you will be disappointed." The absolute certainty etched on his features rocked her back on her heels. His jade eyes glowed, his jaguar close, the duality of his being obvious now she knew what to look for.

"She'll kill us for this," she whispered.

His vicious snarl scattered the humans to a safer distance. "Your sister is dead if she comes near us. I swear it." The surety in his voice made her step into him. Strong arms banded around her, lifting her until she clung to his solid body, legs about his hips and hands hooked around his thick neck.

"I'm not talking about her. Isolde is the least of our worries." She sighed and nuzzled her face into his shoulder. She pulled at the immense heat rolling from his body, drawing it deep to chase away the chill gripping her heart.

He carried her away from the group, leaving the harassed instructor to restore order behind them. His steps didn't falter. Cradling her in his arms, his long legs covering the ground, he strode to the cottage. He kept his hands in constant motion, soothing over her back, stroking her hair.

"I love you, my little salamander. You are mine now, mine forever, and no one will come between us." He whispered the vow against her ear.

She should stop him, make it clear their mating had been a mistake, but she kept silent, wanting to pretend just for a few more moments this could be her future. He crossed the threshold, shoving the door closed with his heel. He carried her to the side of the bed, setting her on her feet. Stepping back long enough to strip his clothing, he turned his attention to hers. She hesitated when he tugged at her top, and he growled low in his throat.

"I need to be inside you, *mi tesoro*. Stop thinking so damn hard and let me love you."

Her clothes disappeared, and gentle fingers turned her body liquid. She needed this, too, needed one perfect moment of unity with this beautiful, brutal creature. A memory to cling to.

Cupping his stubbled cheek, she tugged his face down. Her mouth sought his, sucking at his thick lower lip until he groaned and claimed her, thrusting his tongue deep. He turned them both until he sat on the edge of the bed with her straddling his lap. His thick cock slid through her wetness, once, twice. She lifted her hips and guided him home. The utter rightness of him stretching and filling her body was a unique pleasure. She paused to catalogue every moment of it. The soft, cool cotton beneath her knees, the heat from his thighs, the scratch of the hair on them against her ass. The love shining in his eyes.

He stroked a loose strand back from her face and cupped her chin in his hand. "Mate with me, Ceara," he urged. "Open your soul to me and complete our bond. Make me yours, as you are mine. I love you, *flamita*." He rocked his hips, and she arched her back when his pubic bone nudged against her clit.

"If I mate you, then we will complete the prophecy. The queen will be waiting when we leave the island and our lives forfeit, for she will tolerate no rival to her throne."

Soft lips kissed away the tear rolling down her cheek. His mouth shifted to nibble her jaw then lower to lick the spot where his mark rested. Lightning speared through her body to her pussy. She clenched around his cock and moaned.

"Now you're just playing dirty, you bastard," she muttered, her voice a husky laugh. His sharp teeth grazed the mark, and the muscles of her sex gripped his shaft.

Green eyes blazing, he captured and held her gaze. "Mate me, Ceara. Fuck the future." The press of his fingers on her jaw tightened to the point of pain. "I'm serious, my love. We have four more days on the island. If that's all the time we are fated to share, then I'll take it. But I won't give you up without a battle. I'll fight for you, for us, with all I have. I'll kill for you, raze your clan to the ground to keep you."

She sighed, tracing the thick muscles of her mate's shoulders. If both their gifts were intact, then it might be possible to fight, but what would be the point? She had zero desire to rule. "I don't want to be queen."

He smiled, thrusting his cock into her. "I'm sorry to disappoint you, but you are already a queen. I am the last of my clan, therefore, King of the Naguar." The smile faded, and he grew serious again. "Mate me, Ceara. Four days. Four years. Four centuries. Whatever the Fates have woven into the pattern for us, let us live it to the fullest. Be mine, *flamita*."

The growl in his chest vibrated through her being, and she didn't want to resist him any longer. Reaching deep inside, she gathered her bruised and battered soul, pushing it out. Her beloved mate captured her lips in a kiss of infinite sweetness. The connection between them pulsed, a jolt of electricity shivering through her body. Shim took her offering, surrounding it with his own soul.

His body flexed as though he battled against his shift, and the pressure between them built, stealing her breath away. She hovered on the brink, lungs burning, terrified he would reject her when the horrors of her past were laid bare before him. Their souls entwined, and a sense of peace settled over her. He broke their kiss with a gasp, and she threw her head back. The bond between them rang deep in her soul, filling every empty corner with a love so sure, it humbled her.

Hot lips captured her nipple, and her laughter faltered into a moan of pleasure. He used the edge of his teeth against her sensitive skin, reigniting her passion. Hard hands captured her hips, holding her still while he bucked against her. The bond magnified every sensation, and she knew her mate was right as he drove them both into oblivion.

Four days. Four years. Four centuries. Whatever time remained, it would be enough.

Chapter Ten

Their final days on the island passed in a blur of love and laughter. Shim savored every moment of his time with his beloved mate. If anyone had told him his trip to the island would result in his falling in love, he would have laughed in their face. *The Fates should never be disregarded.*

Stepping out of the shower stall, he wrapped a thick towel around his hips. The portal would be opening in less than an hour, and he had kept Ceara pinned to their bed for every possible moment, reveling in her body until he made them both boneless with exhaustion.

He studied her now, his gorgeous woman standing before the bathroom mirror, lining her luminous brown eyes with a thick kohl pencil. Her battle mask, she'd said with a laugh, laying out the borrowed makeup on the countertop. Stepping behind her, he wrapped one arm around her waist. He wrapped the other around her throat, drawing her head around to capture her lips with his. He ravaged her mouth, claiming every inch of it until she drew back with a gasp of breath.

"Just as well I haven't done my lipstick yet." She smiled, meeting his gaze in the mirror.

The contrast between them struck his heart, her delicate beauty so at odds with the ferocity of her spirit. He remembered the fury in her face and his jaguar exulted. Their mate matched his own dominance. His hand collared her slender throat, the utter trust and love blazing in her eyes reflected the look in his own.

A jagged crack split the mirror. Racking pain drove him to his knees. His guts knotted; fire seared the marrow in his bones. His shift struck, and he threw back his head, crying out in agony. The scream transformed into the jaguar's coughing roar, and his beast surged forward. The sharp scent of his mate's fear drove the jaguar crazy.

He butted her with his head until she sat down on the closed lid of the toilet, so they were at eye level. He rasped his tongue over the mark on her shoulder, the spot his human half had bitten time and again. Ceara belonged to them, and the world would know it.

Nudging his head under her hand, he twisted until she stroked the perfect spot just behind his left ear. Something close to ecstasy flowed through him, and he stretched his tight muscles with tentative care. When the pain of the curse failed to materialize, he relaxed, purring in relief. His mate's scent changed and the worry faded.

Soft hands cupped his thick jaw, and her melted-chocolate eyes shimmered with tears. "You are so beautiful, Shimeer. My mate, my proud jaguar. My black beast," she whispered, and he nuzzled her palm, laving it with his thick tongue until she laughed and pushed him away.

Hope bloomed in his heart. They wouldn't be helpless after all, and he would fight to the death for his mate. Let them come...he would be ready.

Cyrus and Rekkus waited beside the portal when they approached. Shim had chosen to remain in animal form, and Ceara kept pace at his side. She'd woven her beautiful hair into an elaborate crown of plaits. She wore nothing beneath the almost-sheer black dress Sarka had given her as a mating gift. The skirt brushed the floor, and her bare toes flashed from beneath the hem, the nails painted the same blood-red as the tips of her fingers, matching the shade ringing her lush mouth.

His mate looked remarkable, eerie and inhuman. Every inch the Unseelie fae, ready to cut down any foe who dared to come against them. Pride bloomed in his heart. A slight thread of nervousness teased through her smoke-and-spice scent, but nothing in her body language portrayed anything other than surety of purpose.

The Rowans agreed it would be safer for all the other para residents to clear the portal first, so they waited in silence for Rekkus to give them the signal to depart. The big man raised his hand in salute, and Cyrus nodded his head once.

A quiet cough came from behind them, and Shim snarled at the intruder who stood upwind of him. His mate rested her hand on his head, stroking once, and he settled, lowering his snarl to a soft rumble at the small, wizened man smiling at Ceara.

"I was so pleased when you accepted your mating, my dear. Just remember what I told you and everything will be fine."

She frowned at the man, her expression turning speculative, and Shim wished their bond allowed them to communicate telepathically so he could read her mind. She blew the old man a kiss, and he hurried away down the corridor, a rosy blush on his creased cheeks.

Cyrus and Rekkus ordered all the staff of the Haus to keep well clear of the portal just in case.

It was time.

He prowled to the edge of the portal. His mate matched him step for step, her fingertips brushing in light strokes over the fur on his back. The shiny red salamander charm, his key to passing back through the portal, hung from a leather collar around his neck. Ceara clutched a black cat charm in the palm of her hand. Sarka had sworn she hadn't known the significance of his token when she made it, but it amused her to make the cat one for Ceara.

They stepped through, clearing the arrival room without incident. Their feet and paws remained steady, though the ground shook beneath them. They'd barely cleared the portal when the vibrations rose to a crescendo. A loud boom signaled the closure of the portal, cutting them off from the safe haven of the Wiccan Haus.

An honor guard ringed the arrival platform, their elaborate armor designed for show rather than practicality. Shim studied each one, noting gaps between the plates at both shoulder and hip joints. Pointed helms with a slender nose guard and ridiculous black feathered plumes adorned their heads. He flexed his jaw, knowing the thin metal would be no match for the huge biting pressure he was capable of inflicting. A rail-thin woman stood at the center of the platform, her angled form draped in layers of silver material to match the shimmering color of her hair. An elaborate crown rested on her head, a huge emerald suspended from it to dangle in the center of her forehead. She clasped a silver staff in her left hand, a matching emerald set in the top.

Nothing like advertising your position.

Ceara sank to her knees beside him, lowering her forehead to the cold stone in an act of obeisance. She held the position, her red fingernails tapping on the floor until he reluctantly lowered his body next to her. He rested his head on his paws, keeping his eyes fixed on the Unseelie queen. Impatience gnawed at him while the queen stared down at him and his mate for a seeming eternity. His beloved didn't twitch a muscle, although the coolness of the stone beneath them must have been uncomfortable for her.

At length, the queen rapped the butt of her staff once on the floor, and Ceara rose to her feet in a single, fluid move. Instinct told him to place his body between his mate and the clear threat she faced, but he remembered her instructions regarding the way her clan functioned. Any weakness on her part, including him adopting a dominant stance to hers, would be ruthless exploited. He held his position at her side, rubbing the side of his head against his mate's leg.

Her gentle fingers caressed his fur, and the queen let out a brittle laugh. "Tamed to your hand indeed, little Ceara. You have been a very busy girl, haven't you?" Her sharp, high tone was reminiscent of nails on a chalkboard. He curled his lip in irritation. As though sensing his tension, Ceara increased the pressure of her hand, and he subsided with a throaty grumble.

"The Fates have blessed me with a mate if that is what you mean, Ainfean. My mother, my queen." His mate's voice sounded ingenuous as she declared her relationship to the silver-haired woman. Shock rippled through him. *Why didn't she tell me?*

Her fingers clenched in the thick fur behind his head, and Shim turned his thoughts back to the problem they faced. They could discuss his mate's heritage at length, assuming they survived the next few minutes.

"Don't play me for a fool, child!" Ainfean

snapped. "You know that damned prophecy as well as I do. I always knew your grandmother was a troublemaker. I should have ripped Aislinn's tongue out earlier before she had a chance to spew forth such treason."

Grandmother? Shim stared at Ceara in horror, stunned at the benign expression on her face. Not one muscle flickered in reaction. She either already knew about the barbarous punishment, or had been well-schooled not to give any advantage to her mother. *I fucking hate fae politics.*

A crack of noise echoed around the platform, and one of the guards marched forward, summoned to action by the queen rapping her staff on the ground. Shim leaped in front of his mate, jaws wide, roaring his challenge. The guard lowered his spear and ran at him. He bent his back legs, using their powerful strength to launch himself forward, catching the guard high on his chest, knocking him to the ground. The stones ran red as he sank his sharp teeth into the guard's throat, cutting off his scream of terror. He ripped deep, flinging the ruined chunk of flesh. It struck another of the guards with a wet slap on the front of his armor. The man turned a bit green under his helmet, and the jaguar gave him a bloody grin. Abandoning the dead guard, he paced back to his mate. The blood from the fresh corpse seeped across the stone, spreading until it soaked the hem of Ceara's gown.

Ainfean screamed in fury, her staff raised, ready to slam it down again, but his mate threw her hand up. "Hold, my queen!"

The silver staff struck the floor so hard sparks flew from the stone. The remaining guards rushed forward.

Ceara clenched her fist capturing the tiny shower of flames, and Shim let loose another roar of challenge. The guards lacked the discipline to fight as a team. He selected the next one to die, a tall fool who rushed ahead of the others. A wall of flame shot up, cutting them off from the guards, and he reared back, just avoiding singeing his whiskers. Flames writhed around his mate's outstretched hands. She lifted them, driving the barrier of fire higher. A laugh escaped her ruby-red lips, and he roared his approval at the sight of his salamander in all her glory. *Magnificent!* A being of power, and his heart surged at the sight of her.

The guards fell back. Ceara reduced the flames until they danced just a few inches in height. Ainfean, face twisting in fury, pointed her staff at them. A bolt of green lightning burst from the emerald at the top, and he jumped forward, knocking his mate to the ground. Turning his back, he took the force of the hit.

Pain seared along his spine, worse than any he had experienced before, even during the curse. It felt like the meat boiled from his bones. Yowling in pain, the stink of burning hair and flesh filled his nostrils. Shock forced his shift, the unexpected snap and twist of bones adding to his agony. The wall of flame flashed high. Ceara crouched beside him, worry etched on her face. He resisted the urge to vomit. His back felt flayed alive, but he forced himself to his feet. They could not afford to show weakness. His mate's warning rang in his head, and he sucked in a deep breath, locking the pain in the back of his mind.

"I'll live, *flamita*. Let's finish this," he rasped.

His plucky little mate resumed her place beside him, her face a serene mask. Worry and fear laced through their bond, but neither of them would show it. They would give no quarter, no satisfaction to the enemy. The fire faded from her left hand, and he gripped her fingers when she reached for him. The curtain of flames lowered once more, and they faced

Ainfean together.

Ceara spoke, her clear voice ringing out. "My queen, the prophecy is indeed fulfilled. My sundered soul was frozen. I have tamed my black beast." Her fingers flexed in his and he responded in kind. "Our hearts are united and our destiny is upon us. I am queen, as my mate is king. We are the mistress and master of our clan and the emerald lands are ours to rule." Ceara turned to Shim, pride and determination written large on her face. She spoke again. "But our emerald lands are not yours, Ainfean. My crown is not yours. My clan is not yours."

The black cloud of anger on the queen's face softened. "What trickery is this? Do not try to play me, little girl, for I will not yield my throne. I claimed it through spilled blood, and I will hold it through spilled blood, even yours."

Shim stepped forward, drawing the queen's attention from his mate. He suppressed the shudder tickling the base of his spine. Her silvery eyes lascivious, she studied his naked body, the covetous look too close a reminder of the way Isolde had once watched him. A look of possession, of ownership, nothing like the passion and love shining in his mate's eyes. "I am Shimeer Neguar, last of my clan. Long have we dwelled deep in the Ecuadorian rain forest. I am King of All. King of Nothing. My realm is a sea of emerald as far as the eye can see. Ceara is my queen, my mate, my heart. By these words, I declare the prophecy fulfilled."

A calculated look crossed Ainfean's face. She regarded them both, a smile stretching her thin lips wide. "Well, well. You two must be very pleased with yourselves." A scream of fury cut her off, the high-pitched sound echoing around the platform. A blonde woman forced herself between two guards, advancing up the steps to where they stood.

"Bitch! You should have died along with those pathetic humans you wasted so much time with." Isolde screamed again, turning from Ceara to Shim. "You are supposed to be mine. I knew if she died the prophecy would seek to be completed and your resistance to me would disappear." Spittle flew from her lips, insanity glinting in her blue eyes. The madness faded as her eyes rolled back, and Isolde slumped unconscious to the floor.

Lowering her staff, the queen poked the fallen woman in the stomach, grunting in satisfaction when she remained motionless. "If there is one thing I can't abide, it's being interrupted. Now, as I was saying, you two have played a very clever game."

Ceara dropped a curtsey, tugging on Shim's hand until he lowered his head in a stiff bow.

"And you are honestly content to be Queen of Nothing, Ceara?" Ainfean sounded incredulous.

"I am indeed because my mate has given me something you will never understand."

Her mother rolled her eyes. "I had such high hopes for you, daughter, but your heart is as soft as your father's. Please, spare me your prattle about true love and fated mates."

Ceara's laugh vibrated through him as he stepped behind her, pulling her hard up against his body. The need to touch her overrode any sense of self-preservation. He needed her in his arms. She lifted her hand, cupping his cheek where it rested against her shoulder. "Ah yes, there is all that of course, but the best thing my mate has given me is my own volcano to play with."

Silver hair rippling, Ainfean shook her head in amusement before signaling to her guards to collect the unconscious Isolde. "Go and play with your black beast and your volcano, child. I expect to see you at court to pledge fealty." She turned away in a swirl of silver, the guards forming up around her. The procession marched away, and her final cool words drifted back. "Make sure you bring your cubs with you, when you come. I shall want to meet my grandchildren."

Shim spun his mate in his arms until she faced him. She stretched up on tiptoes, and he bent to allow her to capture his lips. The slow deep kiss stirred his cock. He took his time, relishing the sweet temptation of his mate's mouth. She rubbed against him, moaning, and he pinched her ass as he broke their connection.

A wicked gleam lit his mate's brown eyes. "So, what do you think of your mother-in-law?"

He growled in disgust, tossing her over his shoulder. The damage to his back had already begun to heal, his shifter metabolism further boosted by their mating bond. Their bags rested against the portal door, Rekkus having tossed them through before the portal closed. He gathered them in one hand, his other resting possessively on her ass.

"Let's find an inn for the night, so I can show you what happens when you keep secrets from me, *mi tesoro,*" he growled, no heat in his words. Laughing so hard, she almost bounced right off his shoulder. He tightened his grip, flexing his fingers against the ripe cheek beneath it.

Her laughter faded, her smoke-and-spice arousal ripening the air. "I cannot wait, my love."

About the Author

Merryn Dexter is a military spouse who, after a varied employment career (from selling sandals to old ladies with bunions to being a health and safety coordinator for a construction company), is thrilled to be pursuing her dream career as a romance writer. She likes The Winchesters, Spike, Hotch, Loki and watching complicated European Noir. Her hobbies include crying at books, crying at movies, crying at tv serials (there's a theme!) and believes all stories should have a Happy Ending.

Other Books by Merryn Dexter

A Mate's Healing Touch
A Mate's Redeeming Touch
A Mate's Forgiving Touch
Silver Moon
Mating Dance
Boss of Me
Renewed Spirits